WHAT STORMS MAY BRING

PRATITI RENÉE MEHTA

NOTEBOOK
PUBLISHING

First published in 2019 by Notebook Publishing,
20–22 Wenlock Road, London, N1 7GU.

www.notebookpublishing.co

ISBN: 9780993589850

Copyright © Pratiti Renée Mehta 2019.

A CIP catalogue record for this book is available from the British Library.

Typeset by Notebook Publishing.

To Bai

AN AUTHOR'S NOTE

Truth be told, this novel has been in me for years but until this past year, I didn't know if I would ever do it. It wasn't a matter of not knowing what to write or how to write it, but more so a question of whether I could really write something so raw. It was a question of putting all of this on paper, and having it be real, having it be finished; I don't think I was prepared for this to be finished. It was also a question of whether I wanted to write something that bares such a big part of my soul and puts it out there for potential judgment or mockery by a whole world of unknowns. There are the experiences that harrow us, that mold us into people we never expected, and bring us futures we never dreamed would be ours. This is a story of mine: my experiences, my evolution, my future.

Albeit semi-autobiographical, the lines of fiction and reality have been intentionally blurred. If, as you read through the novel, you find yourself wondering what actually happened or whom one of the characters represents, you're missing the point. It isn't about knowing. Each character has been drafted to represent an array of people who have been and/or are in my life. I've learned over the years that every person who comes into your life leaves a part of them behind. Yes, everyone. I am never so much a true representation of myself as I am pieced together by all of the people around me. I have been shaped by my experiences and my interactions, and so every one of those people still lives within me. Some are buried deeper than others, some are in a dreamless slumber, and others actively fight for their voices to be heard. In the end, no one character represents a single person I have met. There are parts of me in there just as much as there are parts of various others.

If I have one hope, it is that having read this you will actively practice empathy. Empathy, to me, isn't always understanding what someone has been through in order to be there for them. Empathy is knowing you will not always understand but are still capable of showing kindness and patience. We always think we know what we would do in a given situation. I include myself in this. In the end, it doesn't matter. If there's one thing my experiences have taught me, it's that we don't know. And that's perfectly fine. In fact, that is the beauty of our existence. We don't have to know. We are all in this storm called life together, sharing one large umbrella. Instead of fighting over it, let's make it bigger. Let's make it better.

Lastly, I want to thank you. Our time in this world is precious, and the fact that you've chosen to spend yours reading parts of my being is of immeasurable worth to me. I hope that the lessons I have learned and shared with you here will resonate, and if not, you will have, at the very least, enjoyed the read.

GHOSTS OF
MELANCHOLY PAST

It was one of those bitterly cold days in Paris; one that makes your bones ache and the ghosts of your past more melancholy. Something stirred in Hélène as she abruptly stopped, finding herself in front of the café L'Artiste on Rue de la Roquette. She still clearly remembered each time she had been here, and given the pain those memories brought with them, decided to sit down on the bench facing away from the café. As the wind bit into her hands, fingers patchy white and red from carrying grocery bags, she retrieved her gloves from her purse and struggled to put them on. The blood rushed back to her fingers as the gloves permeated warmth and provided comfort to her dry, aching hands.

Tears sprang to her eyes almost immediately once the tangible distractions had faded. She could still see traces of her younger self, strolling down the street with him, her delicate hand in his big burly one, eyes full of wonder, joy and dreams of a life unfulfilled until she had met him. Passers-by became blurs as her mind raced back in time twenty years, reliving her not-so-recent yet unforgettable past.

20 YEARS AGO

"It wasn't supposed to rain today," said Guillaume as he exited Hélène's apartment building first to open up his umbrella. "I was hoping to take you on an evening stroll along the Seine," he grimaced. Simply happy to have time with him, Hélène stroked Guillaume's arm reassuringly. They walked for about ten minutes and arrived at L'Artiste, their favorite café in the neighborhood.

The eleventh district had its charms; the hauntingly beautiful Père Lachaise cemetery was a five-minute walk from her apartment, and one could find cozy cafés and restaurants at any turn. Hélène had lived here, on and off, for nearly a decade after her apartment in Montmartre became an impossible location for the peace and quiet she sought. Day or night, there was not a single restaurant, café or brasserie that wasn't catered to or filled with tourists. The real Paris, she felt, was slowly slipping away from her. Desperate to stay connected with the city she had loved more than anything, she packed up and moved. Like all others, this decision was final and unbreakable.

As they sat down in the covered smoking area, Guillaume lit up a Gauloise and inhaled deeply. Hélène found the silver cigarette case that Guillaume had gifted her and followed suit. As they smoked, and she stared into his deep grey eyes, she dwelled on the tumultuous past that had brought them here.

24 YEARS AGO

CHAPTER ONE

Hélène hurried to get dressed as she checked the clock. It was already seven twenty-seven, and she had to be at work by eight-thirty. As she put on her pearl earrings and matching necklace, she checked on her fiancé Eric who was still sound asleep. With a quick kiss on the forehead, she grabbed her bag and left the apartment. One transfer and several stops later, she arrived at La Sorbonne. Having forgotten her umbrella, she ran to her classroom to avoid being drenched. A few minutes early but soaked and frozen to the core, she sipped on her coffee and looked over her lesson plan for that morning.

On the other side of Paris, Guillaume sat in his second train that morning, wondering when Paris would finally build direct lines, so he didn't have to switch trains every day. The infrastructure of the metro drove him crazy; with all points leading directly to the center, you had to cover nearly twice the distance if you wanted to get from one outer corner to another, even if they were right next to each other. Twenty minutes later, Guillaume grumbled about the rain as he entered the La Sorbonne campus.

Two cold and painful hours later, Hélène packed up her belongings, tossed her coffee cup in the paper bin and headed out to finalize her lesson plans for the rest of the day. As she started to walk down the stairs, she slipped and lost her balance. Beginning her fall down the long marble staircase, Hélène's mind wandered to the different stages of her life. But before she could pass the flashes of her childhood into adolescence, something stopped her fall.

Hélène felt the hands on her waist, but the feelings that accompanied this tactile experience were bewildering. It felt as though someone had wrapped her and pulled her close, seemingly into them. She felt an unfamiliar sense of safety and comfort. She processed this new sensation, immensely grateful she had not seriously hurt herself and that this stranger, whoever he was, had saved her.

As he touched her, Guillaume felt not one, but hundreds of sparks course through his body. Despite the brutal cold, he felt as though he was on fire. He wrote this off to the force with which she fell upon him, and the adrenaline likely coursing through his body as he attempted to catch her. Once in his hands, he asked "are you hurt?" while he looked her up and down to ensure there were no signs of blood or broken bones.

Snapping back to reality, she saw the beautiful grey eyes of a man whose face she felt she had known for an eternity. And yet, she was certain they had never met. He had very defined features; a sharp jawline, dark bushy brows that contrasted beautifully with the clear grey eyes, slender lips and stark black hair. She realized she didn't know him, had never even seen him. Still, he seemed every bit as familiar as her reflection.

Guillaume had not yet laid eyes upon her face. It was when she finally said "no, I'm not, thank you,", with a voice as soft as velvet, that he looked into her emerald green eyes. They were big doe-eyes that were rendered even more striking by the long and thick black lashes surrounding them. Her hair was a fiery red, highlighting her eyes that much more. Her face was heart-shaped, with flushed round cheeks and full lips tainted in a blood red. One stray curl hung over her right eye, and as he gazed at her, he lost all sense of where they were, who was around them and anything else that may have been happening.

Hélène was barely able to breathe. She felt his hand on the small of her back; he was helping her sit. She instinctively pulled at her coat when he moved his hand away from her, hoping the coat would provide some measure of warmth. When she finally realized it was useless pulling her damp clothes in closer, she gave the beautiful stranger an awkward smile and thanked him again. She couldn't believe her luck; not only had someone saved her, this man seemed to have stepped straight out of one of those cheesy romance novels you can't put down.

Guillaume was so mesmerized, he almost missed her faint "thank you so much; I'm not sure what would have happened if you hadn't been here." Seated next to her, he smiled and nodded. When she thanked him again, he finally responded. "Of course," he said. "These stairs are quite dangerous, especially in the rain." The rational part of himself returned to him slowly, and once more, he looked over her for signs of any physical distress.

He asked her for her name, which she shared. "Hélène," he repeated after her, and as he did, she thought she noticed something change in him. The warmth that she felt within her moments ago now seemed to radiate from him. She shook it off as her imagination. Not knowing what to say, she sat there silently, eyes darting from him to her feet and finally, to the stairs below them.

Guillaume then shared his name, which Hélène also repeated. It was in this instant she knew she couldn't have possibly imagined what he had experienced. She could feel her heart fall to the pit of her stomach when she said it. There was a sensation, a kind of heaviness that his name brought to her. As she repeated his name in her head, she felt it again and again. She couldn't understand it, considering Guillaume was, by no means, an unusual name.

The rational part of Guillaume's brain continued to reassure him what he was feeling was simply due to the suddenness of the entire scene. While he thought he saw some inkling of a similar sentiment in her, he was first and foremost a man of science. Rational thoughts never fully left him, and so he dismissed the vague and inexplicable feeling as he realized he needed to get going.

Her thoughts were interrupted as he lifted her to her feet. She smiled coyly and thanked him profusely. As they parted ways, she felt the cold seep through to her bones. She knew there was nothing she could do. She couldn't be with him, and strangely, she felt she would never be able to be without him again. Sadly, she had no choice. There was Eric, whom she loved, and whom she would marry in a few months. As she reached the bottom of the stairs, they exchanged one last look, and he turned the corner, leaving her sight.

As he left her, Guillaume felt remorse as he had never experienced it. It was a sensation not unlike saying goodbye to a loved one knowing you may never see them again. He found himself yearning to stay there awhile, if only to gaze at her, but decided he would no longer amuse the ridiculousness his emotions had been condoning. He glanced in her direction, at the bottom of the stairs, one last time. He turned the corner and as he did so, he felt emotions flood him that he could neither entirely control nor dismiss.

CHAPTER TWO

That evening, as Hélène hurried to catch the metro home, she was still dazed and confused by her encounter with Guillaume. She nearly missed her metro transfer, and on the second train, the final ride home, she continued to think about him. His face, his eyes, his safe arms where she felt she could rest her entire life dizzied her mind with an unknown ecstasy.

Guillaume spent much of his day contemplating their encounter as well, and more heavily, what he had presumably felt. He didn't want to validate these emotions, mostly because he couldn't rationalize them. He fought with himself all day, and as he sat on his first train home, he thought about her beautiful face, her full lips he now had a burning desire to touch with his own, and the perfect little curl hovering over her haunting green eyes.

Though he was not seeing anyone at the moment, Guillaume was reticent having had his share of heartbreak. The last woman he had allowed himself to love had devastated him not once but twice, and he swore he would never again allow himself the fragility love warrants. He had, since his first and last love, deemed women to be a distraction, and changing his beliefs now would only deter him from the life he had worked so hard to build. He opened up the newspaper and decided the only distractions he would allow himself would be the news and his academic research.

As she stepped out of the subway and climbed up the stairs, Hélène felt tears rise to the surface. She would be going home to her loving partner, someone whom she felt she had dreamed up. She felt she had betrayed him. She recognized there was no malicious intention to do so, nor was any of this in her control, but the entire walk home, she struggled to decide whether she would say anything at all.

She walked into her apartment, and seeing Eric's face light up, decided it best to forget about Guillaume and focus on her reality - the beautiful one she already had.

CHAPTER THREE

Days turned into weeks and months, and yet, Hélène could not wipe the memory of Guillaume from her head. It had been seven months since that day, and there wasn't a single day since where she hadn't thought about him. She constantly wondered if she had dreamt up the encounter, and if he had really ever existed at all.

Guillaume also struggled to erase the memory of Hélène from his mind. Try as he may, the feeling of Hélène on his hands never left him. The sensations, still raw, followed him day and night despite his constant attempts to make sense of them. There was a moment when he considered letting them take over, but each time his thoughts even ventured in her direction, logic and his previously damaging relationship pushed him to more realistic explanations of what he had been feeling.

Months passed, and in this constant state of battle, Guillaume slowly began to open himself up to the possibility that there may be a way to answer his questions. If, in fact, he saw her again, and the sensations returned, he would be able to analyze them enough to figure out what caused them. He tried not to think of the direction in which this could take him or the potential that he would be breaking his vow to himself. He focused instead on the fact that he hated unanswered questions, and in all his life, Hélène was the biggest question mark he had encountered.

Meanwhile, Hélène's relationship with Eric had begun to deteriorate. Whether it was related to Guillaume or not, she didn't dare ask herself. All she knew was they fought often because of how much she worked. Eric had lost his job, and her absence from their home combined with his extended presence in it usually pushed him over the edge. If all else failed, it was an argument about postponing the wedding because the burden of wedding expenses seemed unrealistic on a one-woman salary, especially that of a teacher. This usually resulted in him accusing Hélène of throwing her money in his face, and eventually, with Eric sleeping on the couch or at a friend's house.

Hélène had started to reach a point where the postponement of the wedding was no longer limited to Eric finding a job. She had serious doubts about how he would handle more difficult situations in the future. But whenever they crept up, she reminded herself she had been emotionally unfaithful to Eric this whole time and had no right to be upset over his not having a job. He had been trying to find something else, and it was all that mattered. Who wouldn't be frustrated without a job and lash out? If there was one thing Hélène did well, it was convincing herself of something and sticking to it.

As the holidays approached and vacations were upon them, Hélène began to feel anxious about being home with Eric. It had been fine during the summer when he had been working, but now with him being home constantly tensions were bound to rise. As she wrapped up her last lesson of the year, she decided she would have to find a way to leave the house for at least a few hours a day under the guise of preparation for the next term.

CHAPTER FOUR

The first day of winter break surprised Hélène. She woke up to a fully cooked breakfast, a clean apartment and fresh flowers. She had nearly forgotten that Eric could be so romantic and caring. They ate and laughed together, then made plans for the holidays. They would go see Hélène's family in Grenoble for Christmas and spend New Year's Day with his family in Angers. They spent the remainder of the day walking around the Marché de Noël along the Champs Élysées, eating freshly roasted chestnuts, drinking mulled wine and laughing. There was so much laughter, it felt like the old days again.

Guillaume usually spent every break he had with his family in Switzerland, but with enough research to be done he decided to stay in Paris. Still struggling to forget Hélène and all he had felt in their chance encounter, Guillaume decided to venture out of his usual spots in hopes of erasing the memories that held him so tightly within their grasp. He convinced himself the reminders were solely a result of repetition, and that if he broke his habits, the mental energy it would take to discover new surroundings and acclimate would surely break the spell.

After researching some of the districts he didn't frequent often, he decided he would venture into the eleventh and spend the afternoon walking around the famous Père Lachaise cemetery. He loved cemeteries; after all, the dead never disappointed. Nevertheless, this adventure, too, failed him. After an unsuccessful afternoon trying to forget Hélène, Guillaume found a well-known café and settled in to do some writing and reading, both of which he was certain would help ease his mind.

A few espressos and many Gauloises later, Guillaume found himself restless. He couldn't comprehend what he was feeling, and forever seeking pragmatic explanations, attributed it to the amount of caffeine and nicotine he had consumed. Continuing to scribe, Guillaume did his best to shake off the sinking feeling that had taken a hold of him.

He finally understood when he saw her walk in moments later. She wasn't alone. From their brief interactions, Guillaume couldn't process whether or not he was her significant other. He stared blankly, dumbfounded by yet another chance encounter and the feelings that swept him, much like they had the first time. He paid close attention, and when he saw the man stroke Hélène's hand and gaze at her lovingly, he felt he had answered at least one question.

GUILLAUME

CHAPTER ONE

When is this damn city going to build a more functional metro system? I'm tired of having to take two trains to get from one part of the city to another, especially when they aren't very far apart. I wish they would finally restructure funding to connect the city in a more efficient way. Whoever thought people would always need to go to the city centre and designed the metro as such clearly had tunnel vision. These thoughts circled my head, like they did most mornings, as I took my connection to La Sorbonne.

The thing about Paris is you never knew what to expect. One minute, the weather is clear, and everything is on time, and the next, you're running like a madman in the middle of torrential downpour because the metro has stopped, and all of the taxis are full of grumbling Parisians rushing to their destinations. One of these days, I thought, I'd have to seriously consider moving back to Switzerland. The benefits would be twofold; one, I'd be closer to my family, and two, the Swiss are known for their efficiency and punctuality.

Anyway, where was I? Ah, yes. The rainy Spring morning passed quickly, and I started the ascent to my second class of the day. Although I had plenty of time to spare, I felt rushed. Out of the corner of my eye, I saw someone slip and begin to fall. I suppose my instinct must have kicked in, though at the time I couldn't tell you what came over me. I can only remember bolting in her direction and catching her before she tumbled further. The minute my hands caught her waist, I felt this yearning, this desire, this wave of inadequacy coupled with completeness. It was and still is the strangest sensation I have ever experienced.

Writing it off to an adrenaline rush, I asked her if she was hurt as I looked her up and down for injuries. She said no and thanked me, which is when I finally laid my eyes upon hers. They reminded me of the wilting grass that finds its last breath of life in the heart of a storm, scintillating like the first dew of the morning. The contrast of the thick black lashes in which they were enclosed intensified them to no end. I finally forced myself out of their trance and helped her sit down. As I grabbed the small of her back, the bewildering sensation I had felt not long ago returned, and I hoped grounding myself would, in some way, help relieve me of it.

She finally thanked me again as she pulled her coat tighter against her body. I could tell she was freezing, which made sense considering her clothes were a bit wet. I responded sympathetically, knowing full well that the stairs were a hazard even when it wasn't raining. I was still taking in her astounding beauty and processing the effect she had

had on me, and it was difficult to take my eyes off of her. I once again checked for any injuries, and with a nagging feeling that I couldn't let myself slip this way, asked for her name. I needed something else to focus on—anything really—so I could stop gawking at her.

Hélène, she shared.

Hélène, I repeated.

It's not a unique name, but the minute the word left my lips I felt sunken. My heart felt heavy and timeless. I can't explain it—I don't think I will ever be able to—but I couldn't stop myself from feeling every ton of the infinitesimal weight it carried. It felt as though all I had experienced in life, all I had become over the years was measured by her name. It was measured through her existence. And for once, nothing was enough; I wasn't enough. I felt weak, immobile, imperfect, all the while knowing only her presence could make me whole again. Nothing mattered but her; I was now a mere shadow of what I had been and traces of what she could make me.

She asked for my name, and I could not have been more thankful for the distraction. As she repeated my name, I saw what I had experienced go through her. I felt every ounce of my emotions run through hers. It seemed inconceivable and beyond the realms of understanding. I couldn't wrap my head around how something like this was feasible, let alone happening to us. As I sat there experiencing the tug-of-war my heart and head were playing, I sided with my head, once again writing off the magnitude of my emotions to a sort of residual adrenaline rush, left over from my leap up the stairs.

I needed to go, mostly so I could try and shake this off. I lifted her to her feet, once again feeling the intensity her touch brought with it. I needed to move on and see if this had all just been a momentary stunning effect; something out of a Sci-Fi novel where you're being beamed up and don't understand what's happening. As we said our goodbyes amongst her continuing gratitude, I felt as though she was taking with her all of the will I had to exist as my own being.

When we parted ways, I felt insignificant, incomplete, incapable, inconsolable. I knew I would never forget this moment, this woman, this feeling, and yet, I wanted to. I needed to. It didn't make sense, and the biggest regret I've had since that moment has been my incessant need to make sense of everything, despite the soul-shattering repercussions. We exchanged one last furtive glance, and with all the strength I have only been able to muster once since that day, I walked away from the woman I have loved every aching moment of my life since I saw her.

CHAPTER TWO

I passed the same staircase at the same time, nearly daily; I never saw her. I had to be discreet, but I was relentless. I did everything in my power to ensure the numbers aligned. The more I passed by the same location, the more probable it was I would see her. By some sick twist of fate, I failed every time. I finally gave up hope and it sunk me into a pit of despair I cannot begin to explain.

I thought of her when I woke each day. When I laid awake in my bed at night, I saw her face until the moment my eyelids collapsed from fatigue. And each painstaking moment of each painstaking day in between, I dreamt of the moment I would see her again. This curse has still not left me. It has lived on in me since the first day, and I think it will until the end of my days. If I knew this back then, there are so many decisions I would have made differently, so many things I would have reconsidered, so many feelings I would have discounted and others I would have gladly embraced. But we'll get there.

It had now been six months, twenty-eight days and fifteen hours since I first saw her face. I didn't know how I could go on without seeing her again. My soul ached from this loss. Every ounce of my being yearned for her and her warmth, for her beautiful eyes to lay their gaze upon me, for her hands to touch my skin. I thought often of her demeanor, her politeness, her apologetic nature. I imagined her to be exactly who she was, of this I was certain. I felt like I knew her and yet, we'd never shared more than names.

The rational part of my mind had started to desert me. As these emotions ran through every inch of me, I tried to fight for a practical explanation. It escaped me time and time again. The last woman I had loved had absolutely and irreversibly crushed me, and I had vowed to never let another woman anywhere near the space I had let her. But here I was, wallowing in my pity and my questions. There were so many questions, none of which I could answer.

GUILLAUME:
MISE-EN-ABYME

CHAPTER ONE

H er name was Sandrine. It was one of those meant to be, knew each other from Adam romances. We grew up together, moved to Paris together, and even ended up in the same university for our post-graduate studies. It's funny; you think that knowing someone your whole life gives you a good idea of who they are deep down. I thought the same of Sandrine. She was my best friend and, at times, my only friend. I had always been more introverted than she, and it had often ended with me blowing off friends for a quiet night of reading at home. Do it enough, and you end up with no friends sooner or later. But I had her and my family, and both had always been enough. I never have and still don't believe in wastefully fluffing up your life with people who add no value, especially when you have no idea how long you'll be here.

I remember visiting the Catacombs when I first moved to Paris. In one of the many sections of skulls and bones, I found a quote that has stuck with me. To paraphrase, it reads something along the lines of: Where is death? She is always either past or future. She is hardly present, and just as quickly as she arrives she is gone. I believe it to be the same with our lives. We measure things by our past and our future, and the present, as it so rarely exists, is gone before we know it. So why would I spend my ever-elusive present—soon to become my past and bring similar experiences to my future—with interactions devoid of meaning?

Anyway, enough about my love of morbid philosophies. Returning to my wretched love story, it wasn't until we were in Paris that things changed. When we first got here, in an effort to be economical, we decided to share a flat. One night, I was sitting in the living room reading, when she walked out of the shower in nothing but a towel. I couldn't tell you if it was the warmth in the apartment or the whiskey I had been sipping, but for the first time, this longing passed through me as I stared her up and down. For the first time in the years I had known her, I noticed how beautiful she was. There was no makeup on her face, her hair was dripping wet, and her towel hugged her curves; I couldn't look away. Catching my stare, she asked "everything ok? You look like you've been stunned. Reading something creepy?"

I didn't know what to say, so I nodded and pretended to go back to my reading. Only, I couldn't focus anymore. I kept thinking about the way she looked, and how I had never noticed it before. Funny as it may sound, until then I had never thought of her as a woman. Especially not as a woman I could date. I'm sure it happens often with friends you've had for a lifetime. It was likely the familiarity and embarrassing childhood moments we had shared. My mind continued to fixate on these thoughts, and I wondered if she ever looked at me differently. While I didn't know it until after it had already happened, I would have my answer in just a few days.

But first, context. Sandrine wasn't the type to get up early; in fact, I couldn't tell you how much we argued about my being a morning person and her hating every part of it. All of our classes started later in the morning (her doing, by the way), and she was usually up just in time to shower before we had to rush out and catch the metro. I called her just-in-time Sandrine, JIT for short.

I, on the other hand, was the type who didn't need an alarm clock unless I had been drinking heavily the night before. The idea of starting my day early was exciting; it allowed me to maximize the time I had to get things done and usually ensured I was free early enough in the afternoon to spend time doing things I enjoyed instead of my scholarly obligations. Also, I loved running, and found mornings in Paris to be the best time to do so. Not many people were about, and there was something magical about watching the sun come up while running down historic cobblestone alleys with their old-world architecture.

A few days later, by some miracle (I later told her this verbatim), Sandrine was up when I got back from my run. She was sipping coffee when I walked in sweaty with my shirt hanging over my right shoulder. As I mentioned, I didn't realize it then, but Sandrine froze. After a delay of a few seconds while I came up next to her to grab a water bottle from the fridge, she muttered a nearly incomprehensible "good morning," set down her coffee mug, and rushed to her room. Not understanding what had happened, I brushed it off and said, "I'm going to go shower first." She responded with an "OK," and we headed to class an hour later. The next few days seemed painfully awkward. I was still thinking about her, and to my surprise the next night, I found out the reason for the awkwardness had been mutual. She had been thinking about me just as much, and to my delight, in the same way.

At dinner the following evening, tired of sitting together like strangers, I finally asked, "is everything alright? Things have been a little strange lately." She looked up for what must have been the first time that night and nodded. A few seconds later, she burst into a monologue that took me a few minutes to grasp entirely.

"No. Actually, it's not. You know," she exclaimed, "you don't just go around doing that. There are rules; erm, yes, rules. You should warn someone if you're going to come in like that. You shouldn't assume someone would enjoy seeing that first thing in the morning, and if you did assume that and you were right, you should think about how awkward it could make the whole living situation thing. But no, who thinks about that? You just do what you want, and then you ask me if everything is alright. Of course it's not! You're my oldest friend, and this, this whole thing, is just plain weird and new, and I don't know what to make of it or how I should feel about any of it! Ugh!"

I sat there confused, trying to piece together what she was saying. It finally hit me that she was talking about my post-run shirtless arrival that morning, and it infuriated me that she was so offended. I understood later she wasn't actually offended, but at the time, I only heard what I thought she would feel. Not to sound vain, but what made this worse was that I was actually in great shape! Also, it's not like I had been dripping sweat all over the floor or that I even smelled. I was furious.

"First of all, I do this every morning. You sleep in, so you never see me, but I have literally not changed a single thing on my end, so I don't understand why I'm bearing the brunt of whatever is going on with you right now. Secondly, what about you? You're one to talk! Pfft! Strutting around, all fitted and hair wet, like that isn't bound to make things weird? We're adults now, and we have to be mindful of what we do around each other. We can't just both walk around however we used to when we were kids. At least I do it when you're sleeping. How was I…"

"Oh, you think I don't know we're adults and we can't be how we were when we were kids? I'm not stupid, you know! We go to the same damn school, we even have a lot of the same classes, and I seem to be doing better than you. So, do not undermine my social intelligence, and for that matter my intelligence or awareness in general, and definitely don't patronize me! I fully understand who we are, and how we are, and..."

I didn't let her finish. The heat of the argument had somehow turned my fury into a desire to have her then and there, and in the midst of her diatribe, I stood up, walked towards her and kissed her. She stood there, momentarily stunned as I had been about a week before, and then moved towards me and kissed me back. And so, it began; after years of a platonic relationship, a romance had indeed kindled, and we fell hard and fast for one another.

Years passed and our relationship blossomed. I loved her. She loved me. And we both had this urgency, this heat to our love. It felt unreal, and as the months turned into years, I still couldn't believe how much we still constantly wanted and needed each other. The passion we shared at night left us breathless, and the love we shared during the day made us stronger. I had begun to think about asking her to marry me. We had had conversations about our future before, and we were both on the same page. We both wanted to get married, neither of us wanted children, and we wanted to work hard while we were young so we could go travel the world in our forties.

CHAPTER TWO

When we graduated, we seemed unstoppable. Top of our class (her scores only a percentage higher than mine), we were filled with limitless potential and immense desire to achieve great things. The best part of it was that we had each other to rely on as we did it. She had chosen an internship with a local firm while I had signed a contract for steady employment, but it never deterred us from being there for one another wholly.

I picked up the ring from a family friend who was a bijoutier, certain she would love it. Young and on the brink of success, I wanted us to celebrate all the wonderful things to come by committing to each other for the rest of our lives. As I walked home, bypassing the subway so I could give some thought to how I would propose, I decided I would take her back to Switzerland so we could see our families, take a weekend trip to Bern and propose to her by the lake. What could be more romantic?

My giddiness started to fade when I started noticing Sandrine had slowly become more distant. My initial reaction was to assume it was the hard work that came with starting any new venture. However, it turned into something I hadn't quite expected. She stayed out late often, didn't phone like she used to do so I would know not to wait up, and often canceled plans because of work. When she was home, there were many work conversations that she chose to take in the bedroom, out of earshot.

Strange as it seemed, I didn't question it, reminding myself we had never both worked full-time before, and that her internship seemed much more demanding than my job. While I spent my weekends at home, she often had to go into the office. I finally understood the saying that distance makes the heart grow fonder, because since she had started working, I honestly missed her too much, and awaited her return home each night anxiously. Given how much time we had spent together since we were young, it only seemed natural.

When we finally got the chance to head out to dinner one night, I said, "hey love, I know it's been really busy for you. What do you say we take a little vacation?"

Surprised at and intrigued by the suggestion, she placed her chin on her wrists and asked, "oooo, where are we going?"

"I think it would be nice to go see my family in Switzerland. And yours, of course. We could take a weekend trip to Bern to get some time away from everything and everyone as well. What do you think?" She seemed happy enough with the idea, and after we finished our meal, we headed home, cheerful as could be.

The next afternoon, she confirmed she could take the time off, and I booked our tickets. We would leave the upcoming Monday and return two Mondays from then. A full two weeks would give us plenty of time to see our immediate and extended families as well as make the most of our four day get-away to Bern. I was ecstatic; we were only a week and a half away, and when the day came, I would be committing the rest of my life to my best friend. My recent concerns over her distance started to take a back seat as I prepared what I would say, trying to strengthen my resolve so that I wouldn't cry mid-speech. Stoic as I could be, my love for Sandrine had been overpowering, and even the thought of our future as husband and wife brought tears to my eyes.

CHAPTER THREE

That Friday, we had planned a quiet dinner at home so we could spend the night looking over hotels in Bern and make a list of what we wanted to do. Sandrine didn't get home at seven as promised, and when I called thirty minutes later, there was no answer. Attributing her delay to the usual bordelle that was her job, I waited patiently. When nine o'clock rolled around and I still hadn't heard from her, I started to worry. I called her again to no avail. I sent her a text message asking her, if nothing else, to let me know she was alive and still at work.

She responded with a simple "yes," which only seemed to make matters worse. In an effort to be understanding—after all, she wasn't there by choice—I decided to read so I would be happily distracted and less annoyed by the time she got home. I must have fallen asleep on the couch for somewhere around three, I heard the front door open. Startled and drowsy, I slowly rose to see who it was. Sandrine came stumbling in, and I could tell from her unsteady gait that she had been drinking. Frustrated, I asked her what had happened and where she had been. Eyes glazed over, without saying a word, she kissed me and went straight to bed.

I spent most of what was left of the night awake, wondering how she could have been so unbothered. I finally fell asleep for a few hours, but given my habit of waking up early, I was up with the sun. I made some breakfast, and unable to find enough energy to go running or focus on any reading, decided to plant myself in front of the TV. Sandrine awoke well after noon with a horrible hangover; when I gave her pain pills and a glass of water without saying a word, she began to explain herself.

"Oh, Guillaume, please don't be mad! I really was at work when you texted, but then, this coworker of mine suggested we go take a break from work and grab dinner and a drink. We were the last ones there and it was so depressing working in an empty office! I had already missed dinner with you, so I assumed you ate. I was starved, and so I agreed. Next thing you know, we were six drinks in without much food in us and had lost the entire evening! I have to tell you, I'm sure my boss is going to furious with me on Monday! Good thing we won't be here!!"

She winked as she said the last part, but I was not in the least bit amused. She sensed my dissatisfaction, and pulling me closer to her, said "look, it was Friday night and we were the last ones in the office. You know I'm not reckless and that I don't just go out binge drinking every weekend. I needed to blow off some steam, you know? It's been so busy, and I haven't really taken a break from it all. And you know me, I love being out. I feel like this job has taken over my life, and I just needed a bit of good-old fashioned, harmless drunken mischief!"

Feeling a bit guilty and charmed by her childishness, I kissed her and handed her some more water. "I know," I said after some time, "I'm sorry. I was just worried and I'm glad you're OK. I'm sure this vacation will be great for us. You can rest; I'll massage your feet and bring you iced tea while you sit there and do nothing. Deal?" Laughing, she pulled me in for a kiss, and for a moment, we melted into each other. We spent the afternoon laying on the couch in front of the TV. At about six that evening, her phone rang and as per the usual, she stepped into the bedroom to take the call.

Some fifteen minutes or so later, she came back out and sat down next to me with her head laying on my shoulder. I asked her if everything was alright. "Yes," she said, "it was just my boss. Apparently he was not amused that the proposal I owed him hadn't made it to his inbox, and considering he was generous enough to approve my vacation, which by the way, were his words and not mine, he decided I needed to be lectured on the value of delivering things on time, how this would never fly at a real job, blah blah blah. I'm pretty sure I tuned him out after the first five minutes." We sat there for another half an hour or so, and I made us dinner. We went to bed early, aiming to be up by nine the next morning so we could pack and get the house ready for the two weeks we would be gone.

CHAPTER FOUR

The next day, when I woke up, Sandrine was already out of bed. Not so surprised considering she had slept a lot the previous day, I headed out to the living room. I didn't find her there, or in the kitchen, but when I walked over to the fridge to get some water, I noticed a handwritten note from her. It read: "Boss called again. Gone for a few hours to wrap things up. Should be back before noon." Sandrine's other notes on the fridge, held on by magnets she collected from every city she visited, made this one seem utterly sad. She had drawn hearts on some, smiley faces on others, plastered declarations of love in all capital letters on most of them and pressed her lips to leave a lipstick mark on a few especially loving ones. Surprised at the lack of a "hi", a proper case "I love you" or hand-written "bisous" at the end of the note, I shrugged and decided to make some breakfast.

I grabbed water, milk and eggs from the fridge and pulled out a skillet for some scrambled eggs. To be honest, I couldn't focus. I kept teetering between thoughts. At first, the lack of Sandrine's usual enthusiasm in her note worried me. After telling myself she had probably left in a rush, my mind wandered to the proposal. Would I propose at sundown? What I would say to her? How she would react? Would she cry? Would I cry despite all of my pep talks in front of the mirror each morning? What if it unexpectedly rained and ruined my plans of a lakeside proposal? From there, my thoughts wandered to our families' reactions, how our wedding would be, who would attend, and while I would have no friends coming to the wedding, how she would have too many and would have to cut her list down. Finally, my mind circled back to her note, and if she had truly just been in a rush when she left.

I decided to go for a run while I waited for Sandrine, and by the time I got back, showered and shaved, she had still not returned. It was already noon, so I decided to call. No response. I sent her a text and asked her when she expected to be home. I got a short reply in return: "probably need a few more hours." Deciding I could cut us some time if I had at least pulled out the suitcases from the cupboard and gathered my belongings, I started to do so. An hour or so later, I had laid out all the clothes I would need, had tucked the ring away amidst socks and underwear in the zipped compartment of my bag, and had the toiletries more or less ready to go.

I threw out all of the perishable food, took out the trash and washed all the remaining dishes. After the apartment was spotless, I decided to take a short nap. Not realizing how mentally drained I had been, I slept for hours; when I awoke, it was seven o'clock.

Panicking, I called out "Sandrine," but heard no reply. She had still not returned. Finally, I called her again, and she picked up.

"Listen honey, I can't talk. I'm sorry, but I don't think Switzerland will happen for me. Or maybe I'll have to meet you in a few days. There's a crisis here and they won't let me go. I'm so sorry. I'll see you later tonight. I should be back in a few hours."

Before I could respond, she had ended the call. Furious, I threw my cell phone on the couch and decided to light up a cigarette. Sandrine hated smoking indoors, so I cracked open a window and decided to blow the smoke out of the window. One turned into a few, and to ensure the full commiseration of my body, poured myself a few glasses of whiskey in between. When she finally returned, I was teetering on the edge of inebriation. I could tell she wasn't happy to find me in this state, but before she could make any mention of it, my tongue ran faster than my mind.

"You know, I've been nothing but understanding. Friday, you said you were working but came home drunk. You're always working. And when you're not, you're always out with your friends. And this trip was the one span of time where we could spend quality time together. First with our families and then by ourselves the following weekend. Don't you want to spend time with me? Why is this internship so important to you anyway? It's not like it pays. Why are you so worried? Just tell them you quit, and we can go on this trip. You don't need to work like a madwoman for someone who isn't even paying you."

I knew I had crossed a line, but if I knew what she was about to say, I wouldn't have felt as guilty about it as I did right after. In a trembling voice she said, "not a real job? What, just because I don't get paid thousands of Euros a month like you do means I don't have a real job? Yes, Guillaume, this is an unpaid internship. But it's going to set my future up for me. I made one irrational decision on Friday, and I paid all weekend for it. But the last person I expected to hear this from was you! And how dare you???"

After a pause to breathe and gather herself, she said, "you don't get it, do you? You don't have friends, you don't like most other people, so you stay at home where you can feed your own ego about how great you are, not needing people who don't add value. What good is the money from your real job and all this intellect if you don't ever go out and use it to live your life? And because you don't have any friends, you make me your whole damn world. I love you, but I don't want to spend every waking minute with you. We've practically done that our entire lives, for crying out loud! When are you going to wake up and realize that not everyone has to be some sort of data or science guru for you to like them or for them to add value? Do you know why I spend so much time at work? So that I don't have to come home to you sulking about how hard you had to work, or how you missed me so much, or how you couldn't wait for me to get home. I want a relationship where my partner can share the joy of their day, what they discovered or what adventure they went on, or even how much they enjoyed some quiet time."

After another pause, she continued. "I just can't see myself with someone who spends their whole life hibernating, removed from the outside world. I want adventure, I want to meet new people, I want someone who does something exciting and inspires me. And honestly, you've only been dragging me down. The more I think about spending the rest of my life like this, the more it depresses me and the more I want to stay out. Coming home has become a burden for me, and it shouldn't be that way. I should be excited to see you, to share things with you and go on adventures with you. But aside from the occasional dinner, when was the last time we did something new or explored a different district? When was the last time you asked me what I wanted to do and followed through? This just isn't working anymore, and I hate saying it, but I was honestly relieved when I realized I couldn't go. I'm at the point where I don't know if I'll even be here when you get back."

I couldn't have been more surprised, and I don't think I ever have been since that day. This fight was one thing, and yes, I had said some awful things, but to learn that she had intended on leaving me was quite a shock. How had I missed it? I thought back to all of the late nights when I waited up for her. She had never once expressed any of this to me, so how was I to know? She seemed happy to see me, glad she was finally done with her day and could spend time decompressing. If this wasn't an ongoing thing, what had so suddenly brought this on?

As I sat there in shock, she folded her arms and looked at me pitifully. I finally asked the question I dreaded most. "How long have you been feeling this way, and more importantly, why didn't you tell me any of this as it was happening?"

She sighed and sat down on the couch. After a few moments of excruciating silence, she confessed, "I didn't know how to tell you. We've been friends for so long, but lately, I just feel like we have grown to be such different people. That's something neither of us could have expected, and while in many cases the differences work, I just can't see them working with us. I've also been thinking about how I rushed into this, not fully thinking about what the future would bring my way. This internship, for example, may eventually land me a job in another country, and the prospect of going to a new place excites me. But," she hesitated, "I feel like I haven't had time to be on my own. When I was home, I was constantly under the watchful eye of my parents. When we moved here, you and I moved here together and well, shortly thereafter, this started.

And now, I feel like the experiences you're supposed to have when you're young and free, when you move to a new big city in search of your dreams, well, I just didn't get to have any of that. Don't get me wrong; I love you so much. You are and will always be my best friend and the person I run home to, but in terms of a relationship, I just need to be on my own. I hope you understand that."

The truth was, I couldn't understand it. When I thought about someday moving out of Paris, I always envisioned doing it with her. "I love you too," I said after much consideration. There was no way I would win this battle; no way I would be able to convince her to stay and give me a shot. Even if I decided to go to Switzerland and give her some space, I couldn't be certain she would be here when I got back. She had said it herself.

"If this is something you feel you have to do, then I can't stop you. I won't stop you. I've only ever wanted your happiness, and as much as I would love to be there on new journeys with you and as much as you're the one I want for all of mine, it's unrealistic of me to expect you to feel the same way. So, go do what you need to; I'm still going to go see my family." When I said these last words, I felt tears well up and my voice broke slightly. As much as I had wanted to stop her, shake her and ask her to snap out of whatever alternate reality she had been in momentarily, I knew there was nothing I could do. I noticed her sniffling and knew she had already been crying.

I couldn't bring myself to look at her; I walked to the bedroom and continued packing. When I finished, I went to sleep. She spent the night on the couch, and the next morning, as I headed out to the airport, she was still sound asleep. That was the last time I ever saw her. The two weeks that followed were painful beyond belief. I spent every moment thinking about how Sandrine could have abandoned me so easily after all the years we had spent together, first as friends, and then as so much more. I hated the thought of returning to the empty apartment, but I also knew it would be the only way I could move on.

CHAPTER FIVE

At the end of the two weeks that were supposed to be the most memorable of my life, I walked back into my now half-empty home. I almost had a foolish sense of optimism that two weeks apart had changed her mind, and I would walk in to find her in tears, apologetic and wanting to start over. Even though I knew all too well how ridiculous my optimism was, I still felt my heart drop as I walked around the apartment.

Every trace of Sandrine was gone; all the notes on the fridge, the magnets she had taken such pride in collecting, etc. Even her towel, shampoo and odds and ends like her bobby pins were gone. My clothes in the closet had been fanned out so it looked like hers had never hung next to mine. She had cleaned any surface where dust might have collected around her objects, surely to cover up any remnants of the space and sense of belonging we had once shared.

It was the polar opposite of a time capsule; she had so carefully removed every piece of herself, it seemed as though she had never existed at all. She had erased years of our history together through the physical emptiness she had left behind. She had done her best to make it seem like she had never been a part of my life, perhaps thinking it would help me move on. Unfortunately, it hurt more than the words we had shared only weeks ago. I spent the day in tears, drinking myself into a hazy slumber. A few more days like this turned into weeks, and after nearly two whole months, even my misery was sick of me.

Time passed, and with conscious effort to rebuild my life and no longer wallow in the suffering Sandrine had caused me, I started to feel better. My healing was cut short when my mother called me from Switzerland. With much hesitation and sadness, she informed me Sandrine was getting married, and that they had been invited to the wedding. Surely, they wouldn't be attending, but she had preferred I find out from her than from someone else. She asked me if I was OK and if I needed her to come visit, but I was utterly speechless. Shock, disbelief and sheer anger took hold, and this was the only time in my life that I hung up on my mother without saying a word.

So, this was her idea of exploring new places alone and being single in big new journeys. It finally made sense; her late nights at the office, her random drunkenness with her coworker. She didn't want to be single, she just didn't want to be with me. Perhaps knowing each other for too long didn't allow for the excitement an acquaintance-turned-romance could offer. Or, maybe living together at the onset of our love had put us a few years ahead of the normal progression of a relationship, not allowing it to organically blossom in the way she may have imagined.

Clearly some form of novelty or excitement was lacking, and with the faults she had not hesitated to list that night, it became obvious: solo adventures had nothing at all to do with her leaving. Everything she had said about wanting to be alone had been a façade so that I wouldn't feel entirely responsible. The part of me that was jaded vowed to never again let a woman's love absorb me to the point of self-destruction. The part of me that was angry wished her marriage would fail, hoping that someday she would realize all she had given up and come running back to me, pleading I take her back.

It took months before my vow took full swing. I spent the time in between as miserable as ever. I didn't eat much, I drank and smoked copious amounts, and I spent time wondering what I could and would have changed. The healing process was painful to say the least; the days seemed longer than ones in the summer, and the nights endless. I stayed awake often, sometimes for days on end, until the rings under my eyes made my coworkers suspicious of my lifestyle and my family worried for my sanity. It wasn't until my mother finally and unexpectedly paid me a visit that I felt a sense of familiarity, of being loved, of feeling wanted.

She stayed for an entire month, selflessly devoting herself to my every need, and when she left my heart broke all over again. Independent as I had become in the years since I had left Switzerland, she was still the only person who loved me unconditionally and made me feel needed. For her sake, if not for mine, I decided to lay off of the drinking and start piecing myself back together. If it wasn't for her, I may have never recovered from the devastation Sandrine had left in her wake. With the passing of my sadness also came a passing of my ill-will towards her. I realized I had healed (as much as I ever would) when I finally hoped that she had, in fact, found happiness, even if that happiness did not include me and definitely did not include being alone.

GUILLAUME

CHAPTER ONE

I needed to get out of my usual spaces. My usual spaces reminded me of Hélène because I had already been thinking of her constantly when I was there. Whether it was the local café or the designated reading area of Shakespeare & Co. with Aggie (a stray cat who had become the bookstore's most famous resident), Hélène was always with me. I couldn't shake it. I picked the eleventh district. With charming cafés at every corner, I was bound to find a place where I could be with no thoughts. I say no thoughts because all of them were filled with her.

I spent the hours of the early afternoon walking around the Père Lachaise cemetery. I had a macabre love of these places; I could think in peace, no one ever disappointed me, and I felt a vivacity that I never felt on the outside. And the graves; I could spend hours wandering around and finding quaint and original graves that took quite the imagination to design. I figured a stroll would do me some good and allow me to refocus my thoughts. Unfortunately for me, all I thought about was her. I couldn't get her out of my head, and the peace I sought escaped me yet again.

After my failed attempt, I settled at the well-known café L'Artiste. The menu had a variety of French and American dishes, and the wine list was impressive. I ordered an espresso to start and slowly inhaled and exhaled my Gauloises. Time passed increasingly slowly, and once again, I couldn't focus on anything productive. I'd come to realize it wasn't possible. The more my mind persisted, the harder my heart fought to remind me of her. I'm sure I gave up at some point and let her thoughts absorb me.

An hour or so later—time had become nothing more than a concept by now, so I couldn't say for sure—the sun was setting. I knew I should head home, but there was something that urged me to stay. Neither hungry nor wanting to drink too early, I ordered my fourth espresso as my ashtray overflowed. Initially aiming to read for a bit, I picked up my journal to pencil my thoughts instead. Maybe writing them down would give them another place to dwell. When I finally stopped to look at what I had written, I realized my journal was filled with the likeness of her. I had drawn her face, her eyes, her beautiful lips, rosy pink and flushed from the cold. I had then moved on to her body, curvy and long, almost dream-like. I proceeded to write her name. Hélène. Hélène. Hélène.

Even writing her name made my heart crumble. I felt like a younger man, madly in love for the first time, hoping that writing the name of my loved one would somehow etch mine into her indelible memory. With every stroke of the pen, the passion with which I wrote grew fiercer, and I found my ink bleeding on to the next page. In mind, I had only the hope that I would find her again. I would finally answer the questions that constantly taunted me and, to be fair to my rational mind, attribute these "feelings" to nothing more than the excitement of the circumstances under which we met.

I was scribbling her name for the hundredth time when every part of me froze for a few seconds, and a kind of restlessness took over my soul. I tried to understand the source of my inertia; maybe it was the crash from the multiple espressos or a nicotine overdose. Better yet, maybe the fatigue brought on by my incessant questioning had finally caught up with me. I realized what this was shortly thereafter, when I saw her walk in with a man I hadn't seen before. Gravity expanded tenfold. I couldn't move, speak, breathe, scream; I was completely depleted of my free will.

CHAPTER TWO

I paid close attention. I didn't think she had noticed me, but I found out soon enough. I saw her adjust her posture, then she turned around and met my eye. I smiled, and to be honest, I was surprised I had been able to do so in my state of continued disbelief. I didn't want to say or do anything in case she was, in fact, with him. I turned my gaze quickly and went back to writing. I saw her turn around and say something to this man, but I couldn't quite hear her.

I kept a close watch; I was careful to not stare for too long, inadvertently drawing his attention when it was really hers I wanted. I caught a few affectionate touches, and despite not wanting to believe it, I had an overwhelming feeling that they were more than friends. I saw her laugh, the kind where one throws her head back and laughs with the entire body. I saw her reach for his hand; she seemed happy. I wondered if I had imagined what we felt in our first encounter, and if despite its fading voice, the level-headed man in me had tried to warn me to not get carried away. Had this all been a figment of my lonely imagination, desperately seeking a genuine connection?

As they finished their meal, the only thing I remember thinking is that I had to know, once and for all. Maybe then I would be able to go back to the life I knew; a life of comfort and hope for a resilient future. The minute he got up to head inside, I took the only chance I thought I may ever have. I approached her, and after a few polite hellos and how do you dos, asked her if they were married. She said no, but they would be the following year.

To explain how I felt in this moment is something I am still not to do. I don't think any language could do justice to the pain I felt and the disappointment that jolted my heart in its cradle. Despite my earlier assumptions about forgetting her once I knew who this man was, I knew forgetting her would be akin to forgetting how to breathe or walk. Somehow, this stranger had become such a big part of me I couldn't break the cycle, how much ever I may have wanted.

I don't know if I said anything to her. I just remember walking back, and even if you didn't know me, I'm sure you would have assumed I had just received devastating news. It would be a lie to say I have never since experienced such a graveness of the soul, for I did it to myself time and time again. But we'll get there eventually. All I can tell you is that not even the last woman I loved before Hélène had such a profound impact on me, despite us having been together for years.

I sat back down and as much as I wanted to leave, I couldn't. I stayed and watched her fidget with her bag as she pulled out some change for the bill the server had just dropped off. She had the most seemingly delicate touch; the way she picked up her bag, then pulled her wallet and the cash filled me with an envy of the objects around her. Never had I imagined I would be thinking of Jacques Brèl's Ne Me Quitte Pas; never did I dream I would ache to become the shadow of her shadow. As I gave in to the despair I felt, I saw him return.

What happened next still shocks me. I had never seen someone treat another person this way, let alone someone who had done nothing wrong. He slapped the money away as if her hand would contaminate anything it touched. I could tell she was hurt as she massaged her hand and looked up at him, and yet the shock did not allow me to move. I sat there, furious and shaken, wanting so desperately to help and yet entirely unable to do so.

After loud, hate-filled words that likely crushed her, he stormed off. All at once, my mobility returned to me, and before I knew it I was picking up the money off the ground. Having returned it to her, I went inside to pay the bill. When I came out, she was ready to leave. As much as I had wanted her to stay, I couldn't muster the words to tell her. I couldn't manage to assure her that it would all be OK, and ask her if she wanted to stay, have a cup of coffee and talk. She was crying, and amidst her multitude of apologies, I never got the chance to ask.

She left me before I could say a word, but I couldn't move, unable to comprehend what had happened. I walked out to see where she had gone, but she had disappeared in the few minutes I stood contemplating. As I laid in bed that night, I felt like a helpless fool. What if he had done something worse to her when she got home? What if his anger had amplified and not meaning to do so, he had seriously hurt her? I didn't even know her family name, let alone her address. I wouldn't know where to find her. I kicked myself time and time again for letting her walk away and spent most of my night this way.

CHAPTER THREE

I tossed and turned in the early hours of the morning when it suddenly came to me. People had recognized them and said hello as they walked in. Even if she wasn't a resident of the immediate neighborhood, she did seem to frequent the café often enough. I would have to go back. Of all the times I have been grateful for my painstakingly detailed left brain, this was the most momentous.

Showered and ready, I headed out to catch the metro. My timing, albeit unplanned, couldn't have been more perfect; I walked in right as the café was opening. Considering no one was there that early, I was able to sit at the same table I had night before. In the back and facing the entire room, it was easily the best spot in the house to people-watch. And this way, I would see her as soon as she walked in, if she did at all.

I felt her before I saw her, which by now was a clear pattern. I could no longer deny that her proximity burdened me physically as much as it did emotionally. As soon as she walked in, she looked at me. I noticed she didn't have to look around the room to find me, and I surrendered. There was clearly something between us that connected us in the way I had suspected.

CHAPTER FOUR

y head was racing. Maybe it was my heart. I was curious about all sorts of things. I wanted to know what she liked to do in her free time; if she was studying or teaching at La Sorbonne; if she was well read, and if so, what some of her favorite works might be; if she enjoyed movies; what kind of music she loved the most. And there it was. My rational brain creeping up, trying to hint at obtaining every little detail about her so some material fault of hers could allow me to deem her unworthy of my affections.

Meanwhile, the internal tug-of-war continued as I wondered what she was most passionate about, and how she manifested this passion into action. I'd always defined people by the tragedies that brought them to tears, by the things that moved them, by the purpose they felt they had on this earth, if they believed in any purpose at all. I wanted to know what she thought of déja vus, of coincidence, of fate. This part of me yearned to understand her philosophy, her way of life, and the ideals she pursued in her life. I realized I didn't actually care about her favorite color, season or song. What I cared about was why she loved all of those things, what they meant to her.

Speechless and intoxicated by her presence, I let myself walk without direction. We ended up at Père Lachaise, where we must have walked for hours. I wasn't really sure how long it had been since we had left L'Artiste. It took everything in my power to refrain from physically running into her. It wasn't clumsiness or any sort of inability to walk in a straight line. I was drawn to her. I wanted to hold her hand or at least brush her shoulder so that I had some semblance of physical contact.

At times, I pretended to look at the graves in amazement. Other times, I simply purposefully walked away from her. I wondered for a while if she thought I was repulsed by her. A few times, I was sure I saw her intentionally walk at a distance from me. If she wanted to leave, I suppose she could have. Maybe she thought the same of me. After much wandering and trying to keep oneself apart from the other (or at least it seemed that way), we exited the cemetery and walked out into the street.

CHAPTER FIVE

Still having uttered not a word to one another, we kept walking. It must have been an hour or more, when a sudden downpour forced us into a small brasserie. There we ate and stared at each other some more, again without any sort of verbal communication. The only time she spoke was when we ordered, and I realized she didn't eat meat. It amazed me how easy it was to spend hours with her without saying a word. The comfort these silences offered astounded me. We were able to say everything we felt to one another without ever moving our lips. I noticed a pained expression on her face, and once again, her silence told me what it meant. I asked if I could see her again, but instead of responding, she got up to use the restroom.

When she hadn't returned nearly ten minutes later, I started to worry. Fidgeting with my silverware, my eyes were glued to the staircase leading to the restrooms. I saw her head pop up, and a sigh of relief washed over me, though it didn't last long. She looked different somehow, shaken, scared. I straightened my posture as she walked up, and then I noticed it. There was a scrape on her face that only became clearer as she came closer, cuts on her hands, the beginnings of a bruise on her right arm and a few spots of blood on her dress.

She must have read my expression and explained it was no big deal; she felt fine. I insisted we stop at a pharmacy, and it was only then that the outside world came back to us. Not having paid attention to anything but her the entire night, I hadn't noticed the roaring thunder and the pouring rain. The server informed us that no pharmacy would be open in this weather. Most businesses had already shut down for the night in anticipation of flooding and metro closures.

We exited the restaurant, and with the urgency I felt to find a pharmacy close by, if at all possible, I started to pick up the pace. When I noticed she wasn't beside me, I felt like an inconsiderate ass. Of course she couldn't walk as quickly anymore. She probably had scrapes and bruises all over her body, and my rushing would only cause her more pain.

I slowed to match her pace, and she asked to stop for a moment. I complied, and she pulled out her phone to type a message. I had a feeling it was to her fiancé, but I didn't ask. The only concern I had was to clean her wounds before any sort of infection set in. Once she was done, we walked around to a few different pharmacies in the area, but there was no sign of an open one anywhere. The only things we had gotten out of this search were soaked legs, nearly up to our knees.

At this point, I turned to Hélène and asked if she had any medical supplies at home. I had no sooner asked the question than I realized what a terrible idea it was. I didn't know if she lived with him, but considering they were only months away from the wedding, it was highly probable. I restated my thought to ask if I could take her to the nearest hospital, but she insisted it wasn't as severe as it seemed. Out of any other viable options, we agreed I would clean and dress her wounds at my apartment, then get her home. She agreed, and we started to walk again.

With the neighborhood being familiar, I kept my focus on Hélène. I watched her face closely as she walked, ensuring I could spot the slightest indication of pain. She seemed lost in thought, and despite my concern for her, I wished I knew what she was thinking. I wanted so badly to know what had been running through her head. Mainly, I wanted to know if she was thinking about him or me. I dismissed the idea that it could be me, blaming my narcissism. Whatever it was, I wished she would share it with me. It would help me understand the person with whom I was already wishing to spend a lifetime, the person about whom I knew so little and cared so much.

CHAPTER SIX

I unlocked my door, helped her sit down and leapt to the restroom for my first aid kit. I pulled out antiseptic, some gauze, a cicatrice ointment and some bandages. I noticed her tights and directed her to the bathroom so she could take them off. As she did so, I could hear her gasps of pain. I went to the door and asked her if she was ok, to which she said yes. When she came out, I helped her sit back down.

I was about to start with the left leg when I noticed a black line creeping down her thigh and stopping just beyond her knee. She explained it was a tattoo. Without being prompted, she mentioned it was a poem by Baudelaire that talked about the ecstatic union of sound and light. While I didn't need the explanation considering I knew the poem very well, I was amazed to hear her describe it. She had to have loved it; it had to have been an ideal in which she whole-heartedly believed. Why else would she have marked her body permanently? Here it was at last; this is what I had wanted to learn about her all day. Clearly, this poem had moved her. My heart became more inquisitive; this small window into her soul had made her an even bigger mystery. I longed to hear more, but when I realized she was done, I returned to taking care of her.

I slowly cleaned each wound with disinfectant, and with ample warning that it may sting. I didn't see her flinch once. After all the wounds had been cleaned, I put on ointment and gauze before sealing it with a bandage. I asked her often if what I was doing hurt, and each time, she responded with a no. Once I was done, I started to check metro schedules. With delay warnings at every possible route, I turned to her and asked if she would like me to get her a taxi home. She conveyed her fatigue and unwillingness to go anywhere, so I headed to my bedroom to change and find her something more comfortable. I would sleep on the couch so that she could sleep on my bed. More than anything, I wanted to ensure her discomfort didn't aggravate her injuries.

When I came back out, she was laying down on the couch. I handed her the pajamas, and she headed to the bathroom to change. In the time she was gone—and for the first time since I had met her—I noticed her scent, which had filled my apartment. It was a sweet perfume, and yet, it wasn't overwhelming. As I opened up the couch into a sofa-bed and sprawled out, I inhaled deeply.

She walked out wearing my pajamas, and if it was possible, I think I fell for her even more. While the pants fit her in length, the shirt was a bit too baggy, and the sleeves a tad too long. Drowning in the oversized top, she looked small and fragile. While I laid there smiling, she did not look one bit amused and her expression had changed significantly.

I was confused, and before I knew it, she was demanding to go home. The sudden change in demeanor frightened me, and I asked if I had done something to upset her. As I nearly jumped up off of the couch, I saw her grab her tights and stuff them into her purse. Her body must have felt the shock of her quick movements, for a second later, she sat down on the edge of the sofa-bed. I urged her to let me know what I had done and apologized as sincerely as I possibly could have for having offended her. Once again, I told her that whatever it was, I didn't know I had done it.

She took a deep breath and explained. She didn't understand how I could've expected us to share a bed. Yes, she felt our connection, and yes, she had spent the entire day with me, dined with me and even came home with me. But she had only done so because of her current situation and it didn't mean I could take advantage of her. She was hurt by the type of woman I took her for, and if I thought I could treat her this way, I was terribly mistaken. I'm sure this wasn't the best response, but I let out a laugh, which only seemed to upset her more.

She looked at me in astonishment, and I explained I had already made my bed for her since she would be more comfortable there. I would sleep on the sofa bed. I could see the blood rush to her cheeks. Unclear as my intentions had been, she had completely misunderstood them, and for this, she apologized (once again) profusely.

As she slowly rose to head to the bedroom, I walked over to the kitchen, filled up a glass of water and grabbed two painkillers for her to take. I advised her it would help reduce some of the pain she was bound to feel the next day and would be grateful for it in the morning. Come to think of it now, there was no way for someone to know. If you don't take them, you wake up in a world of pain, yet there would be no point of reference.

I digress. Back to Hélène; she thanked me and went into the bedroom. As I settled back on to the sofa, I couldn't help but think about how cute she looked when she was mad. Yes, I know. Of all my wordiness and ability to articulate beyond the average, the only word that came to mind was cute. I imagined her asleep, and what an angel she must resemble. As my mind focused some more on her sleeping, I decided to ensure she had everything she needed to be comfortable.

I got up and knocked on the bedroom door. A few moments later, I heard her faintly tell me I could come in. I didn't enter; I opened the door slightly and let her know there were extra blankets on the left side of the closet, should she feel cold. I also asked if she needed the heat, which she mentioned she did. I bid her goodnight, shut the door, and immediately started the central air. It was one of the things I loved most about my apartment; I didn't have to wait a while for the desired temperature.

As I drifted off to sleep, I wished that I would, someday, have the joy of sleeping next to her. If my assumptions about her were correct, as they had been thus far, she would be nothing short of angelic. The thoughts lulled me to a deep slumber where I dreamt of her mesmerizing eyes, of my hand in hers and of her in my arms. I dreamt of touching her lips with mine and feeling her breath on my skin.

CHAPTER SEVEN

The next morning, like every morning, I woke up early. She was still sound asleep, so I decided to go for my daily run and pick up some breakfast. I pulled out a new toothbrush and a fresh towel from the cabinet, and placing it next to the sink, added a note stating I would be back soon. As I ran around the fifteenth district, new fears filled the pit of my stomach. I ran faster knowing there was a possibility I would come back to an empty apartment. I didn't want her to leave without saying goodbye; in fact, I had already decided I would drop her to her doorstep. I wanted to spend every moment I could with her. The man was still in her life, it seemed, and if this was the last time I saw her, I didn't want her to leave without a proper goodbye.

By the time I had finished my run, my t-shirt was soaking wet. I stopped by the boulangerie on the corner, picked up some bread and croissants, then ran to the Monoprix for a few different cheeses. Running back to the apartment, I skipped the elevator and ran up the five flights of stairs. I was relieved to walk into my apartment and find her belongings on the dining table. She was still sleeping, so I took off my shirt, washed my face and hands, and began to set up breakfast.

A few moments later, she walked out into the living room, freshened up and smiling. She wished me good morning, which I returned breathlessly (this time from my run more so than from her, though the effects were about the same). She looked away almost immediately, and I realized I was covered in sweat, most of which was still running down my chest. Embarrassed, I headed to the bathroom to shower immediately.

When I walked back out, I brought over the breakfast to the dining table. As I set it up, she thanked me for what she called the "magic pills" from last night, which had helped her walk without excruciating pain this morning. She sat down, picked up a croissant and nibbled at it slowly, trying to avoid crumbs. I found it endearing how careful she was being, and she must have noticed my smile, for she smiled back as she finished it. After breakfast, I removed the now dampened bandages, and cleaned and dressed all of her scrapes and cuts again. Once this was done, I knew I could no longer avoid the inevitable.

We headed to the closest metro stop. I got ready to scan my pass, but she insisted she could head home on her own. Selfishly, I tried to reason with her, making up excuses about her injuries and being worried about her going back on her own, but her hard-headedness outdid mine, and we parted ways. As I watched her scan her ticket and cross to the other side, I felt a sharp pain in my chest. I waved to her, and soon she walked out of sight. She didn't look back once.

HÉLÈNE

CHAPTER ONE

I've never believed in soulmates. Actually, I should say I never had believed in soulmates. Until I met him. I can see the day as clearly as the wrinkles under my eyes and the lines on my palms. It was rainy and cold despite the beautiful spring we had hoped was here to stay. I remember regretting the fact that I had left my umbrella at home. I was running late, and with tardiness, I was and still am prone to forgetting at least one thing. It never fails me.

The metro was my thinking space. After all, I had taken it enough to know my transfers and stops inside out. For me, the thought that morning was Eric. It was almost always Eric; our future together, the upcoming wedding, the way I pictured he would look at me as I walked down the aisle. I was thrilled to be his wife, and more so, to start a life with a wonderful man after years of betrayal and disappointment.

I really hated that I had forgotten my umbrella. As I surfaced the streets, I realized this was more than a slight drizzle. Once again, my inability to leave my bed early enough had cost me. I would've run to campus, but I would've been drenched either way. And honestly, I always did love the rain; I still do. It's one of the reasons I can't imagine living anywhere but Paris. Whether it's an unexpected summer shower or an expected winter storm, the rain has a magical effect on the city.

Paris comes alive in the rain. The streets are grey and cold, but the trees come to life, and the warmth of the bars and brasseries amplifies tenfold. The same espresso that fuels your body on a warm summer day becomes an antidote to the bitter cold and fills you with a sweet warmth. It becomes a quintessential part of one's being. The Indians have chai, and the Parisians have espressos. The rainy weekends by the fireplace are my favorite. With a good book in hand, there's nothing like enjoying the view of a drenched Paris in cozy pajamas, sipping a freshly brewed coffee while the fire roars and its embers spark.

As I entered the campus, I was relieved. I headed up to my classroom, arranged my affairs and sipped on my coffee given I had a few minutes to spare. Students were bound to be late on account of the rain, and frankly, I was grateful. Rainy days were harder because I longed for my books, my tea and my fireplace.

I gathered my belongings at the end of the lecture, which is when I realized I hadn't finished my lesson plan for the rest of the day. I rushed out to the library in hopes that my hour long break would give me enough time. I didn't want to scramble in front of my afternoon class; they were the toughest group of all. As I headed down the beautiful marble staircase, I lost my balance. It was likely the rain, but I can't be sure.

All I knew was that I was falling, fast. I was nowhere near a handrail, so at this point I knew nothing was going to stop me. However long I fell, and however hard, I would just have to deal with it. And in this moment, I started having flashbacks of my childhood. I saw my parents and a younger version of me. I was happy, laughing and running around while my parents joined in the laughter and kissed. Before my mind could jump to my adolescent years, I felt it. At first, I thought the heat was a byproduct of my body hitting something, the precursor to pain or my body's way of preparing me for it. I was wrong. I realized it was a set of hands on my waist, preventing me from falling further.

While I felt the hands, that's not what I felt. I know; I'm not making any sense. What I'm trying to say is I felt warmth. I felt comfort. Can someone even physically feel comfort? I felt like someone had wrapped me in a cocoon of warmth. I kept trying to comprehend what I was feeling but believe me when I say there was nothing in this world that could have prepared me for it.

His soothing but assertive voice broke my spell. He asked if I was hurt, and when I looked at this stranger, I was immediately captivated by his eyes. Grey, profound, perfect. So was his entire face. He had slim lips, his jaw was sharp, and he had dark, thick eyebrows that matched his jet black hair. I knew I had never seen him before but there was something about him that seemed uncomfortably familiar. I felt connected to him somehow, and yet part of me screamed that he was a total stranger.

After losing myself in his eyes for what felt like an eternity, I could barely get out the words to tell him that I was OK and thank him. I tried to pull my coat over me tighter, and it had to have been years before I realized my damp coat was only making things worse. In all honesty, it may have only been a minute or two at most. Try as I might, I couldn't understand the timelessness I felt. It felt like the world consisted of nothing but the two of us; I had never felt more out of touch with reality.

Feeling overwhelmed and at a loss for anything else to say, I thanked him again. I couldn't tell him what I was really thinking. I didn't even know his name, but I was exhilarated with these new sensations he had evoked in me, and I was petrified of his effect on me. I felt I had known him for a lifetime without ever having met him. I found myself staring blankly at him as these thoughts continued, and my face flushed with embarrassment.

He reassured me. Something about the rain and the stairs. I was barely gathering myself when he spoke to me again. This time, he asked for my name. I told him. As he repeated it, his demeanor changed. To what, I couldn't say. I just felt it. Something shifted within him, but it wasn't like the gentle rustling of leaves in the wind. It was as if mountains had been moved, painstakingly and magnanimously. I thought I was going crazy; maybe I had hit something after all. The rosiness in my cheeks only worsened as I realized I had been silently staring at him again. To break the tension, I asked him for his name. It was in that very instant I understood everything. It wasn't in my head. I felt it.

Guillaume.

My heart sank to the depths of my soul when I said it. It seemed impossible. It's a common name. It's just a name, for crying out loud! But before I could process it any further, I felt his hand on my back. He was helping me stand up. I didn't have time to say much besides muttering a hundred thank yous. He didn't even look at me as he walked away. It was definitely possible I had imagined it and projected what I was feeling onto him. A second ago, I could swear his soul was on fire and now, I couldn't feel anything at all except for cold.

I gathered my composure and walked down the stairs, watching my every step. As I reached the ground, I looked up and saw him turn the corner with one last look in my direction. I knew that if I never saw him again, I would be devastated. And if I did, well, my life would be. I walked on to the library as planned. The rest of the work day was a blur, and each moment that inched closer to the last hour of classes filled me with more dread.

On the entire ride home, much like the entire day, I was unable to shake Guillaume from any part of me. I felt a sort of elation when I thought of him. What ensued was guilt. Guilt for the sensations I had never experienced with Eric, guilt for what felt like emotionally cheating on the love of my life. I exited the metro to catch my connection just in time; a second later, and I would have had to backtrack.

As I exited the station to begin my walk home, tears sprang to my eyes. I couldn't understand what had happened to me, and more importantly, why it was happening now. We were months away from our wedding and this stranger had arrived suddenly, disrupting our lives. I knew I didn't want any of this to happen. I didn't wish for any part of it. I felt the dread resurface when I thought about what I would tell Eric, if anything. Maybe he could help me process this. Or maybe, and more likely so, he would be heartbroken.

I don't remember the walk home. As I turned the key in the lock, I saw Eric's face. He beamed as he welcomed me home, and by the loose tie hanging around his neck, it seemed he had just come home as well. I knew I couldn't tell him. Why would I throw away this life we had built for something I couldn't even explain? No, I wouldn't tell him. After all, nothing had really happened.

CHAPTER TWO

It had been months and Guillaume still hadn't left my thoughts. I wondered everyday whether I would see him again, knowing full well I had changed my route so that I didn't run into him. I was afraid of what may transpire if I did. I couldn't see him, and yet, a part of me hoped for divine intervention. I know we mustn't wish for things. The universe has a way of bringing things our way, and I have always believed that I can manifest my thoughts into reality. Say what you will, but it's happened to me more times than I can write off as mere coincidence. I felt conflicted and torn inside and out. I couldn't be with him and life without him had been miserable thus far.

Maybe it was just the fact that Eric and I had been fighting more. I didn't dare ask myself if we were fighting more because of what had happened with Guillaume. All I could say is that since Eric had lost his job, tensions had been rising. I don't know how he could have thought that I would ever fault him for a company shutting down and for him not being able to find another job. I would never want him to work somewhere he wouldn't be happy. Surely, he knew that. We all say things we don't mean when we're upset.

And yet, he thought I believed all of these things. He hated that I was never home. He didn't like me paying for things because it made him feel like less of a man. The wedding was another sore subject, despite my efforts to gently explain that with him not working, the cost of a celebration was one we just couldn't bear. I tried to explain that marrying him had been a dream of mine since I had met him, and it wasn't willfully that this postponement had happened, but my words fell on deaf ears.

Perhaps Guillaume had stuck with me because of all of this. Maybe he was my canvas. On him, I could splatter dreams unfulfilled and fantasies about the man of my dreams. On him, I could draw the nostalgia of my early days with Eric, when we were so happy. On him, I could etch the desires I'd since repressed. Maybe this, too, would pass. One day, when things were better again, Guillaume would be but a fading impression of the things I had with me all along.

There were just too many maybes. If only I had a clear answer. My mind was exhausted. If it wasn't from teaching, it was the dialogue I had with the other part of me. The part that missed him and secretly wanted us to run into one another again. The part that wondered if things would change when Eric did get a job and worried the postponement of the wedding was no longer conditional to him finding one. The part with too many maybes and no certainties.

Where I should have been focusing my energy, however, was what I would do during the next two weeks. Eric had become more irritable over time, and while I had dealt with it because I was away most of the day, I would not have the same luxury during the holidays. I needed to find a way to leave the house. I would use lesson planning or research as a guise, but whatever the excuse, I knew I would have to get out. I couldn't imagine walking on eggshells the whole time, afraid anything I say would set him off.

CHAPTER THREE

I woke up the next day and I could've sworn I was still sound asleep, dreaming. Eric had cleaned the apartment (I don't even know when; I didn't hear a thing), gone out to get fresh flowers and made us breakfast. I was stunned. I couldn't believe this was the same Eric who would blow up at any given moment and sleep on the couch or spend the night at a friend's house. Sometimes, he would be gone for a few days until I filled his voicemail with apologies and pleas to come home.

Maybe things were turning around for him. Just maybe, we could go back to the life we had; one where we were happy, where I was solely his as he was mine. We enjoyed breakfast, laughed, and I could certainly say this much: for the first time in months, Guillaume had escaped my thoughts. We made plans. We would go see my family in Grenoble, his in Angers and then spend some time in Paris at the tail end of the holidays. I was ecstatic. I couldn't remember the last time we had made plans like this. Nor could I remember the last time we felt so light-hearted, so happy, so free of the burdens that had consumed us for months.

We spent the day at the Marché de Noël, picking at roasted chestnuts and enjoying the warmth of mulled wine. We felt euphoric, free of stress and optimistic about our future. It really had been the perfect day, and so reminiscent of our early days together. We had made it a tradition to visit the Marché every year, and while I hadn't even been sure we would go this year, I much less imagined it would be this wonderful. As the sun set and turned the sky into a beautiful harmony of gold and orange, we headed back to our neighborhood. I had lived here for a few years after I got sick of the hundreds of tourists constantly flooding my previous residence of Montmartre. As sad as I had been to part with the heart of artistic inspiration, I wanted the real Paris. I didn't want a souvenir shop on every corner or overpriced cafés and brasseries. I wanted peace, art and culture, and the eleventh district had it all.

We entered the café L'Artiste, one of our regular dining spots. The evening staff we had come to know so well greeted us, and we headed to our usual table. Once I had settled, however, something made the hairs on the back of my neck stand up. It felt as though someone had inserted a rod along the length of my body; my back stiffened like I had never experienced. Not knowing why, I turned around, only to find my grey-eyed stranger seated directly behind me. A few moments passed, and when I turned back around, I knew Eric had seen the exchange. I explained Guillaume was a coworker and returned to looking over the menu.

I could feel Guillaume's stare even though I wasn't facing him. I knew he had been watching us, but I didn't know if he had seen Eric's affectionate touches. As I adjusted myself to block Guillaume's view, I felt tremendous guilt. In efforts to push it away, I did all I could to be present with Eric. After all, he was my fiancé, and we were eventually going to be married. No stranger would change that. We talked and laughed some more as we ate our meal, and again, for some instants, it's as if Guillaume had never existed.

When we finished our meal, Eric headed to the restroom. Before I could turn around, Guillaume was standing next to me. After strained hellos, he asked if Eric was my husband. I mentioned we were engaged and planned to marry the following year. He walked away without a word, and I could only imagine how I would have felt in his position. He walked with a weight I shared. A weight of remorse for something we would never have; one that has never left me.

I returned to my reality, and when the check arrived, I rummaged through my bag to find my wallet. I counted the bills, then put my bag down and started to place the money on the table. Before I could reach it, Eric had slapped my hand so hard I felt a stinging sensation. I looked up at him with tears in my eyes, and I knew what had happened before I ever heard his words.

After the perfect day, after a glimpse of what we once had and still could have had, we had come back full-circle. Once again, the fact that I was paying made him look bad. I made him feel like less of a man. I made him feel like he wasn't doing enough. And before I could say anything, he had walked off. It had all happened so fast. With all eyes on me, I tried to gather myself and collect the money, but I couldn't move.

Guillaume was by my side before I realized it. He picked up the money, returned it to me and took the check inside. When he came out, I had been able to gather my belongings and with a hundred apologies, much like the hundred thanks I had given him during our first encounter, I ran out. He didn't chase after me, and I could tell he was just as stunned, if not more. In this moment, and probably for the only time in my life, I wished we would never cross paths again.

CHAPTER FOUR

I waited for Eric most of the night. No calls, no texts, and when I tried reaching him, radio silence. Since he lost his job, Eric had not once afforded me the courtesy of a conversation. It was always an argument, and it was always about what I did to make him feel a lesser man. I wished more than anything, that his mindset would change. I couldn't stand the thought of what might happen if we faced bigger hurdles in the future. I didn't know if our marriage could withstand trials and tribulations like losing both jobs, our home, or worse, a child. I feared all of it would somehow be my fault again, and that I would forever be a scapegoat for his insecurities.

My eyes felt heavy from an entire evening of crying, and somewhere around three-thirty in the morning, I decided to sleep. I could smell him on our bed sheets, and it devastated me. I don't remember when the tears stopped, and the dreams began. The next thing I knew, it was nine in the morning, and there was still no sign of him. Somewhere in the night, a heavy downpour had begun. It was still going, and I decided I needed caffeine. I showered and dressed and knowing full well the morning staff at L'Artiste would be different, I headed down to the café for a quiet morning of reading.

Before I even entered, I felt the same sensation I had felt the day before. This time, however, I didn't have to doubt or try and understand it. For a second, I wondered if I should go to a different place, or if I should just go home and wait for Eric to return. For a second, I thought I had a choice. My moments of hesitation hadn't stopped my feet from carrying me in, straight to Guillaume's table. He looked up at me the instant I entered, as though he had been expecting me. I didn't know what to make of it, but now that I was there, I would at least try and explain what had happened the night before.

I asked him if he was alone, and I was happy to hear he was. I sat down, and without asking him how he was or if he had someplace to be, I started running through the events of the prior evening. I explained Eric wasn't as bad as the incident had made him seem. I explained I was difficult and thoughtless at times; how I would sometimes unintentionally upset people. Finally, I explained I wasn't the easiest person to deal with, and that with my many quirks and how picky I was, I could...

His hand on mine stopped me dead in my tracks. I was tongue tied and frozen, yet I felt as warm as a summer's day. Everything I had felt in our first interaction rushed back to me, and I couldn't so much as remember what I had just said. We stared into each other's eyes for what seemed like ages. Our spell was only broken when the server came to ask for my order. I asked for an espresso, and we continued locking eyes until my espresso arrived a few moments later. In utter silence since his hand had touched mine, we sipped and smoked.

There was a moment, at the end of my espresso, when I stared into the empty cup that I realized I shouldn't have been doing this. As a dutiful fiancée, I should have been at home, trying to reach and console Eric. While I had been thinking about what had happened to me, I had completely disregarded how Eric must have felt. Given how much we frequented this place, other regular patrons knew and recognized us. Surely, the fact that I always paid would have raised questions in their mind and painted an image of our relationship that wasn't fair to him. I needed to find Eric and talk to him.

The other part of me, the one that has never left me since the day I met Guillaume, didn't agree with my need to put my life on hold for someone who had broken my heart time and time again. I wanted more time with Guillaume. I needed to see if this was real, if this could be something, if we could be something. We still hadn't talked, we knew nothing about each other, and maybe once we did so, we would realize we had built the other up in our heads. Except, I knew very well I hadn't. I tried to tell myself it would happen, but I already knew the more time I spent with him, the more I would fall irrevocably in love with this man and there would be no way out.

I was relieved of my indecision when we walked out together. I didn't know where we were headed initially, but we ended up entering the Père Lachaise cemetery. We walked for hours. I'd always told Eric I wanted to be buried here. I loved this place. I still do. The solitude, the peace, the changing of the seasons. It's ethereal. And being here with him; well, I can only say it made this place all the more important to me. We tried our best to not be completely absorbed by one another. Sometimes, I would move a bit to the side; other times, he would catch himself nearing me and move away.

Hours went by without either of us realizing it. When it neared closing time, we walked out together. Without a destination in mind, we turned the corner and kept walking. It could have been days instead of hours, and I would be none the wiser. It felt like it had been ages, but it still wasn't enough time. The rain, which had cleared up earlier, came back with a vengeance. Before long, we were forced into a local brasserie for dinner.

We ate, once again with silence and stolen glances. His smile was beautiful. It lit up the room. It lit up my soul. I'll never forget his smile. There was an innocence there; it made him even more irresistible. He mostly had a serious expression, so the few times he smiled, it set my soul on fire. As we spent more ages together that flew by in instants, it neared ten in the evening and my heart sank to my stomach. I knew at some point I would need to go home.

Not only would I have to explain where I had been to Eric, I also dreaded what would come of the conversation if he wasn't as interested in how I had spent my day. I had come to appreciate the expression damned if you do, damned if you don't. I worried the worst was yet to come, and the day before was but a glimpse of what he had bottled up inside. My worried expression must have read clearly on my face, for Guillaume finally asked if he could see me again.

CHAPTER FIVE

I was speechless. I didn't know what my future held. If I went back home, I didn't know if I'd be allowed to leave the house until school reconvened. I didn't know what to expect from Eric. I still hadn't heard from him, and as my mobile phone showed no messages or calls from him, I worried I would have yet another lonely night in store. Only this time, my lonely night would be filled with thoughts of Guillaume and the pain of separation. I know Guillaume was still waiting for an answer, but I couldn't find the right words to express what I had been thinking.

I headed to the restroom to prepare myself for my journey home and find a way to answer Guillaume's question. As I thought about what a perfect day it had been, once again, I felt myself falling. Only this time, I was completely out of sight and there was no saving me. As I fell, I remember trying to feel for the handrail. I couldn't find it, so I braced myself and covered my head with both hands to protect myself from any major damage.

Minutes later, I found myself still agonizing in pain. I managed to get up, and sobbing, I sat down on the last step to gather myself. I noticed scrapes on both of my knees under my tights, and I noticed a stinging in my right arm. Both of my hands burned as well. I finally found the strength to get up again, splashed my face with some water and slowly headed back to the dining room.

As Guillaume saw me walk back already concerned, his look turned to sheer panic. He must have noticed my limp, and so before he could bombard me with questions, I tried reassuring him I was fine. He only grew more and more worried. He urged us to go to the nearest pharmacy, which is when I finally recognized my obliviousness to the outside world. The server explained nothing would be open considering the flooding.

In all my life, I swear I have never missed a thunderstorm. I'm always aware. Whether it's the flashes of lightning or the roar of thunder, I listen intently. After all, it's my favorite weather. Somehow, the time we spent at the brasserie locked me in a sensory vacuum, for I heard and saw nothing. I hadn't noticed the place was empty, I hadn't noticed the urgency on the servers' faces, and I certainly hadn't noticed the screen in the background reporting flash floods around the city. Most importantly, I had missed the leak from the top of the stairs that led to the loo. As we paid the check and stepped out into the thunderstorm, I also realized I was a long way from home.

CHAPTER SIX

As I struggled to walk at my natural pace, Guillaume slowed down and locked arms to keep me safe. I felt the safest I have ever been in my life. I asked him to stop for a minute, and when he did, I pulled out my mobile phone. I typed a message to Eric: "gone to a friend's, will be back in a day or two." I didn't write I love you or kisses as I normally would've done. Given he had not even bothered to check in, my fury with him grew, and I decided I would let the storm in my heart guide me tonight, wherever it may decide. We resumed our walk, and after stopping at a few pharmacies and getting drenched up to our calves, Guillaume asked me if I had any medical supplies at home.

Before I could find the right words to explain that my place wasn't the best idea, Guillaume seemed to have had the same thought and retracted his question. He suggested we go to the nearest hospital, and I assured him that wasn't necessary. I didn't think I had injured my head and a couple of scrapes didn't need a visit to a doctor. He then suggested he take me to his place, which was close by. This way, he explained, I wouldn't have to walk much, and provided the metro was still running, he could take me home when we had cleaned my wounds and I had gotten some rest.

I agreed somewhat reluctantly, dreading where this could lead us. We didn't walk for much longer, and before I had realized it, we were headed to the fifth floor in an elevator. It was a nice building on the inside, freshly painted and newly renovated. As we exited the elevator, he led us to the left and turned the key in the corner apartment, which opened up to a small but cozy one-bedroom.

CHAPTER SEVEN

After helping me settle onto the couch, he ran into his bathroom to grab medical supplies. While I took in the alternating grey and white walls and a few pieces by Dali and Magritte (my favorites) on the walls, I saw him come back out with disinfectant, gauze, an ointment and some band-aids. Seeing that I had tights on, he offered use of the bathroom so I could take them off. I complied.

The bathroom was simple and neat as I imagined it would be. That was the recurring theme of his apartment. Everything was simplistic, but traces of his personality could be found everywhere. Despite looking like someone actually lived there, his apartment was so tidy I was afraid of moving anything out of fear he would know. As curious as I was about him, I didn't want him to think I had been snooping through his things.

When I started to take off the tights, I realized the blood had stuck to them, and as I ripped each one off of each knee, I grunted in pain. Within seconds, he was at the door, asking if I was okay. I responded with a yes, and I heard his footsteps recede.

I returned a short while later with my tights rolled up into a ball and sat back down on the couch. Guillaume squatted in front of me so he could clean up the bloody mess on my knees.

He stared at the vine creeping down my left leg onto the knee, and I explained it was an excerpt from Les Bijoux by Baudelaire. I summarized it by stating it was only when light and sound came together did one's soul fill with ecstasy and a furious love. He looked into my eyes as he listened, but I couldn't tell what he was thinking. He turned back to my knees and with a warning it may sting, began to clean my wounds.

I was so mesmerized by the way he was taking care of me, I hardly felt anything at all. His focus, his attention, his concern were all appealing in a harmless way. I felt safe with him. I felt like he could cure all of my wounds without ever needing to see them. I don't know what it was exactly that caused these feelings to arise, but here in the home of a stranger, I felt safer than I had ever felt with Eric.

What burned with every wound wasn't the antiseptic. Every time his skin grazed mine as he put on a bandage or applied the ointment, my heart gushed with warmth. Even though I knew he couldn't sense what I was feeling, I was sure my cheeks were flushed from embarrassment. He kept asking if what he was doing hurt, and I kept saying no. The truth was, it did, but not in the way he had meant.

When he finally finished, he went over to his phone and started to look up a route home. He informed me that there were severe metro delays. Given the time, it was likely I would wait for hours without no guarantee I would even catch one before they stopped running altogether. He offered to call me a taxi, but I confessed I was exhausted, and that the thought of going anywhere at all seemed unreasonable. He understood, and saying nothing further, retired to his bedroom.

I n his sudden absence, I decided to lay down on his couch. There was a blanket at one end, which I grabbed and laid over me. Without my warm tights, shivers ran down my spine, and the lack of heat in his apartment had only made it worse. I heard my phone buzz, and when I opened it up, I saw Eric's name flash on the screen. I sprang up and as my muscles ached from the jolt, so did my heart.

The message read, "I'm sorry, my Hélène. I don't know what came over me. I don't know what comes over me in these fits of rage, and I know that you don't deserve it. I promise to be better, and I understand that you need space. Take the time you need, but I'll be here, waiting for your return. I promise we'll go back to how things were. I know the storm is raging outside, but if you need me to come get you, I'll grab a taxi in a heartbeat. Love always, Eric."

CHAPTER EIGHT

A few moments later, as I sat there flustered and confused, Guillaume walked back out in his pajamas with a spare set in hand. I closed my phone, gratefully took the pajamas and headed to the bathroom to change. When I came out, I found him lying on the couch. Still thinking about Eric's message and seeing Guillaume on the now pulled out sofa bed made my head ache with rage.

I told Guillaume I wanted to leave, and as he sprang up, more confused than I had been seconds ago, I started to gather my things. As the pain coursed through my knees, I was forced to sit down. He sat down next to me and asked me to explain what had happened. In my fit of anger, I shut down as I always do and refused to talk. He insisted he would be happy to take me home if I wanted, but that he really had not meant any offense with anything he may have said or done and reiterated his lack of knowledge as to what had happened.

After a few deep breaths, I accused him of assuming we would share the couch. Yes, we had an amazing connection that was inexplicable, and yes, I had spent the day with him, had dinner with him, and hell, even come home with him. But did that mean that I would spend the night in his arms? If he had thought that's the type of woman I was, well, he had thought wrong, and we would never see each other again. I demanded he call me a taxi immediately.

I was shocked by his laughter. He explained he had arranged the bed for me so that I could sleep comfortably. He would take the sofa bed, and in the morning, he would take me home. I felt like a fool. This man had taken care of me, cleaned my bloody wounds, and here I was accusing him of being sleazy. I felt ashamed and humiliated, and after apologizing repeatedly, I got up. He gave me two pain killers and some water, assuring me I would thank him for it in the morning.

Downing the pills and gulping down the water, I headed to his room after I bid him goodnight and apologized yet again. His room was (surprise!) neat and simple. There was no clutter, and his open closet showed neatly pressed shirts, organized by color. The pants were on the bottom, also arranged from lightest to darkest. The tones were mostly whites, greys and blacks, and I assumed these to be his favorite colors. My hands grazed some of his clothes as I peeked at them closely.

His nightstand had a copy of the Harvard Business Review, a gold chain, and a photograph of him with his family. His sister made a funny face and looked quite animated, while he wore his usual serious expression. His parents were both smiling and seemed happy. He really seemed to be the one out of place, almost unhappy. As I wondered about his family and their history, I heard a knock on the door. I sat down on the bed before asking him to come in.

As he stood by the door, refusing to enter, he let me know there were extra blankets on one side of his closet should it get cold. He also welcomed me to wake him up so he could turn on the heat, or he could do it now if I felt I would need it. I took him up on his offer. I'm always cold. It was true then, and it's true now. He said goodnight, and within a few minutes, I heard the roar of the heater as warm air started to flood his room.

I slept more peacefully that night than I had in months. I dreamt of us. We walked hand in hand, and although I don't remember where, we were happy. We had a life of our own. Eric didn't haunt my dreams that night, though I did feel a nagging feeling that what I was doing to him was inhumane. If he ever found out that the "friend" I was staying with was this man, the one who made me feel all of these things, he would surely never forgive me. Our relationship, suffice it to say, would be over.

My dreams didn't care. My dreams only sought out Guillaume, with his perfect jawline, his deep and captivating stare, his strong hands and perfect posture. Drool covered the pillow when I awoke the next morning, and I turned it around in hopes he wouldn't notice. I sat there for a while, reveling in knowing life could be like this. I knew I wouldn't be waking up to uncertainty, to temper tantrums or hissy fits, but to my wonderful stranger with whom I had spent the most wonderful day.

CHAPTER NINE

I headed to the living room, but there was no sign of Guillaume. Thinking he may have run down to get breakfast, I decided to freshen up. There was a note taped to a new toothbrush, wishing me a good morning and letting me know he would be back soon. Next to the toothbrush was a towel, which I assumed was for me. I brushed my teeth and showered, and as the hot water doused me, I felt the sting of my wounds and the bitterness of my time with him ending.

I got dressed and came out to find him in the kitchen, shirtless. It seemed he had just come back from a run, and as beads of sweat rolled down his perfect abs, I looked around the room, careful not to let him see my jaw hit the floor. He excused himself and walked past me to the loo, and I have never been more grateful he didn't stick around and try to have a conversation. If he had, it would have surely been one-sided considering my words had failed me altogether.

When he returned, he had showered, and was fully dressed in a button down and jeans. He started cutting up a baguette and laid out some cheese and pastries as he asked me how I felt. I told him I was a bit sore but that it was manageable, and he smiled in return. I thanked him for the pain killers as I attributed my ability to walk at all to the magic pills he had given me last night.

He brought what he had been preparing over to the small dining table in the corner, and I realized he had a whole spread; three types of cheese, a couple of marmalades, and a few croissants. I picked up a croissant and ate it slowly, carefully avoiding any crumbs from falling on to his table. He smiled as he watched me eat, and I smiled back realizing how silly I must have looked.

After breakfast, he removed the wet bandages he had placed on my knees the night before and started to the clean the wounds. As I inhaled sharply, he put one hand on mine and told me to squeeze it as hard as I needed. Truth is, I didn't need to anymore. As soon as his hand was in mine, I don't remember feeling a thing. He bandaged me up again, and we headed out to the nearest metro stop.

I told him I could take it from here, but he insisted he could at least drop me to my doorstep. After several minutes of reassuring him that I could get home just fine, he let me go. As I inserted my metro ticket and passed the gate, I looked back one last time. There was that wretched remorse again, and despite a distance of only some metres, I felt as though we were oceans apart. I waved goodbye, started walking towards my platform and didn't dare look back.

CHAPTER TEN

When I entered my apartment about thirty minutes later, Eric was pacing. I greeted him, knowing full well that this was not going to end in my favor. I had learned to recognize the signs. He never smiled when he was in this kind of mood, nor did he acknowledge that I even existed. The pacing was the biggest sign that he had a lot on his mind, and that I would bear the brunt of it. Not surprisingly, I was grilled about where I had been, exactly who this friend was, and how I could have left him alone. I think at this point, I had finally had enough.

At first, I tried to reason with him; after all, he was the one who had deserted me. He scoffed, which was more infuriating than him accusing me in the first place. I persisted, telling him he had no right to ask me where I had been after the way he had treated me. Not once, I articulated, had I asked him which friend he spent the night with the multitude of times he had deserted me. Not once had I expected him to apologize for his anger and hurtful words, even when I knew I had done nothing to instigate.

He rolled his eyes and said nothing to me the whole time, except to interrupt what I was saying with laughter. When I finally lost my temper, I stormed right back out of the apartment, leaving him alone with his pride. After all we had been through, after all of the support I had provided and how understanding I had been, I couldn't believe how he had acted. I wondered what had happened to the man I fell in love with years ago, if he had always been this way, and if it was just the first trials of our relationship that had brought out his ugly side.

I walked into my beloved cemetery, hoping the walk would clear my mind. As I tried to lose myself in the maze that was Père Lachaise, my mind wandered to Guillaume. He had never asked me about my relationship with Eric aside from wanting to know if we were together. And yet, there was no judgment in his approach with me. He didn't assume anything, and his behavior towards me never changed. I thought back to our day together, our time in this very cemetery, trying to keep away from one another.

CHAPTER ELEVEN

I exited the cemetery and walked over to my favorite cocktail bar, Lone Palm. As I crammed my legs into one of their amusement-ride looking booths, I ordered drink after drink, trying to figure out what to do next. I didn't want to go back to the apartment and face Eric, and I had no family in Paris on whom I could call. Even if I did, I don't know that I would be able to explain why I needed, so desperately, to be away from him.

Families were like that. As happy as they were for me, I knew that they worried about my tentative nature. I knew they hoped he was the one, and I would finally settle down. Backtracking now would only earn me their disapproval, and I couldn't have that. I hadn't shared with them what had been happening since Eric lost his job, and my sudden arrival would only raise questions I didn't have the courage to answer. Answering them meant accepting my reality, and it was the was one thing for which I wasn't quite ready.

Yes, I had met someone else, but I also knew they would never believe if I said it had nothing to do with him. They wouldn't believe I had been battling Eric's demons for months now, and that there were several instances where I had to talk myself out of leaving. I didn't have the courage to do it up until now. Not because I didn't have Guillaume before this, but because I worried about disappointing my family. Sure, it could all have been in my head, but only time would tell. I knew at this rate, I was bound to have the conversation with them sooner or later. Later would have to do.

Drink after drink arrived, always the same Palm Springs cocktail that I loved so much. I delved deeper into how I would ever begin to explain what had happened for months now to anyone without arousing suspicion that I had ulterior motives. By the time my last drink arrived, I was positively wasted. I could feel it in my inability to stand up to go to the restroom. I asked for some water, but the damage had already been done. By three o'clock in the afternoon, without any food in my system besides my morning croissant, I had downed six potent cocktails.

I managed to get up, pay my bill and walk out. I don't know where I was headed. I walked around without direction, and yet, somehow my purposelessness had guided me to the metro station. I let my heart guide me and started my journey to him, still heavily intoxicated. By the time I got off at his stop, the alcohol and my nerves had become fast friends. As if the amount I had already drank wasn't enough, I stopped at the first brasserie I saw for one more.

Mid-way through my first drink, I looked up and realized I had found my way to the one where we had dined the night before. The nerves kicked in full-force at this point, and one drink turned into a few. I didn't dare walk down the stairs to the restroom (as much as I had wanted to check how red my face was by then). I took down each drink easier than the last, and with a fresh dose of drunkenness, continued my journey to his apartment.

By the time I got there (I should mention it was a blessing and a curse to not forget anything), I could feel how hot my skin was to the touch. The alcohol had stopped coursing and was now sprinting through my veins, and my fear had left me. Not knowing the code to get in, I rang his apartment. No answer. I rang again, and I still heard nothing. I wondered where he could be and sat down on a nearby bench to wait for him.

GUILLAUME

CHAPTER ONE

I headed back to my apartment, defeated. It was one of the times I wished I worked over the holidays; I could have used the distraction. I must have read the front page of the newspaper at least seven times, and each time, I remembered nothing. I kept picturing her, and with her smell still lingering in my apartment, it became impossible to think of anything else.

I decided to go for a run. It would help me feel as though I was moving on, albeit only physically. As I ran around my district, I thought of her even more. I would have to fill my day with something so that I wouldn't get depressed thinking about her absence. I came back to my apartment, showered, and then decided to head to the Pompidou for another attempt at the much-needed distraction.

As I neared the fourth district, however, I was hit with a wall of despair. I entered the museum and wandered, never really remembering what I had just seen or where I was headed next. This went on for hours, and by three, I needed a drink. I headed to the Bar Hemingway in the first district and ordered the drink I usually only ordered after a funeral or a heartbreak - the infamous Death in the Afternoon. A deadly concoction of champagne and absinthe, there was nothing better to help you forget your sorrows.

Or drown in them indefinitely, depending on your state of mind.

I gulped down the first one, immediately regretting it. In my quest to be healthier, I had sworn off drinking on a regular basis. In fact, I couldn't remember the last time I had had a cocktail, let alone one this strong. The pain felt slightly dulled by the heavy dose of alcohol, so I ordered another, and then another after that. By the time I left the bar, I was definitely sloshed, which meant sleep would come easy. As I headed home, I thought more about Hélène, and it rose desires in me that had long been dormant.

The ride home was a blur. I remembered seeing the infamous old lady who screams at anyone and everyone for food and money. I shifted uncomfortably as she passed me by, never directly looking into her eyes. That was the trick; if you happened to mistakenly make eye contact, you were bound to have more attention than your fellow travelers. I practically stumbled up the metro stairs, and as I did, I thought I faintly smelled Hélène's lingering perfume.

When I approached my apartment building, I noticed the goosebumps under my coat. In my drunken state, I thought I was imagining things, but as I got closer, I was relieved to find otherwise. My clumsy stranger was seated on a bench outside, gazing aimlessly into the street. She turned her head when I walked up, and without a word, we walked in together. As we rode up the elevator together, the overwhelming stench of alcohol on my person became more and more noticeable.

It wasn't until she tripped and stumbled walking out of the elevator that I realized she was equally if not more drunk than me. I made no mention of this, but it relieved me to know I wasn't alone. As we settled on the couch, she asked me what my poison of choice was. She looked horrified when I told her, and I couldn't help but laugh. She laughed as well, and I felt at ease. Her presence always had this effect on me; I was finally able to relax and reveal my whimsical side. No one ever saw this side of me, and it was a relief to let it out.

CHAPTER TWO

We talked for hours, and what I said I still can't remember. I must not have spoken much, because there was a moment when I remember her asking me why I was such a closed book. The truth is, I wanted to share everything with her. I was just so drawn in by everything she said, that all I did was listen to her. She spoke of her love of poetry, why she was in love with Rimbaud, why she went to Charleville-Mézières once a year and dropped off a letter to him, why people laughed at her when she talked about it.

She told me about her childhood troubles, her tendency to dream of the most ridiculous things and how so often, people had to remind her to step back into reality. We shared life philosophies, and I learned she was, without the shadow of a doubt, a Surrealist. She spoke so passionately of these things; it was hard not to smile. I remember her stopping several times to ask if she had said something funny. She hadn't. I was enamored by the glimmer in her eyes as she spoke of the things she loved. It was hard to miss and harder not to fall for her more and more with every word. I finally had the conversations I wanted; I understood the how and why, not just her likes and dislikes.

We opened a bottle of wine and drank some more. Before we knew it, it was two in the morning, and neither of us had a desire to stop. She suggested laying down so we would be more comfortable, and so I pulled out the sofa bed. We laid down, drank, talked and laughed some more, never taking our eyes off of one another. I could have stayed there forever. Every part of me was hers, and by four, we started to feel the effects of the long day we had had.

I told her she could take the bed again, but without saying a word, she got up and laid out her hand for mine. I gave it to her, and we walked into the room together. We fell asleep rather quickly, but about an hour later, I felt her shaking. I had forgotten to turn on the heat, and with the storm in full swing, the apartment had gotten chilly. I tried getting up to turn on the heat, but she pulled me in closer.

As I put my arms around her—the first real intimate contact we had had—I felt light-headed. It could have very well been the amount of alcohol in my system, but this was a different high. I felt as if I was floating while I cradled her and held her close. My body always ran hot, and she sighed as she stopped shaking. A few minutes later, she turned around and faced me. As she looked up at me and thanked me, I nodded slowly.

Our faces were the closest they had ever been, and my nodding resulted in my chin hitting her top lip. She kissed it softly, and before I could understand what was happening, our lips were locked. We kissed for a long time; hours, of this I'm certain. From time to time, I would stop to look deeply into her eyes and tell her how beautiful she was. Every time, she would thank me by kissing me more passionately than before. We swam in the oceans of each other's breaths for as long as we didn't need our own, stopping every so often to catch them.

Our bodies felt the full weight of our emotions, as did our souls. As much as I wanted to experience the full length of the passion I felt, I respected her. We fell asleep again after a few hours with her dress unzipped and my shirt unbuttoned. As she laid across my bare chest, I knew this is how I wanted to spend every night for the rest of my days. In my euphoric state, there had been no thoughts of her fiancé or their impending marriage.

CHAPTER THREE

The next morning, I woke before her to make some coffee and arrange something for us to eat. She stirred when I left the bed, but quickly fell back asleep. I washed my face, brushed my teeth, and headed to the kitchen. It wasn't long before she joined me. She asked me to zip up her dress, and as I did so, I gently kissed her neck. She turned around, smiled and kissed me with the same passion she had all night. I got us our coffees, and we sat back down on the sofa-bed. I asked her how she had slept, and she said peacefully. After some small talk, she mentioned she would have to leave soon.

I immediately regretted asking the question, but I needed to know. She said his name was Eric, something I didn't want to know. She said they had fought again yesterday, and that this time, she had finally had enough. She was sure this wouldn't last; he had become an entirely different person. They had been fighting for some time, and each time, it escalated.

There was something about her situation that didn't quite sit right with me. I asked her if she was going back today to call off the wedding, and she said she wasn't sure if he would even be home. She never answered my question directly. Surely, she had felt what I had felt last night. And therefore, surely, she wanted to pursue this. How could she not? My demeanor must have changed, because she asked me if everything was OK. I nodded and took our empty cups to the kitchen.

She put on her shoes and grabbed her bag. I walked her to the metro station, and as we parted ways once again, I felt more broken than I had the last time. On my walk home, I felt torn. Part of me wanted this woman with every ounce of my being, while the other quickly realized that I was taking her away from someone else who was bound to love her just as much. However he had been acting with her, there is no way this man would want to lose her. I realized I may have been standing in the way of someone else's love, and it hurt me to see the man I was becoming.

My mind then wandered to the night before and new questions arose. Had she come here not having ended anything with Eric? Was she testing how she felt about me, or was she just lonely? If she really felt the same way, why had she not decided to end things? Why had she not definitively stated that was what she was going to do today? As these thoughts swarmed me, I felt more and more restless. I didn't know when I would see her again, if ever. I wasn't certain she would come back to me. Maybe I had just been a buffer, a nice little fling while she figured out how to make things work with Eric.

HÉLÈNE

CHAPTER ONE

I knew he was approaching me, and I turned my head to meet his gaze. He looked as handsome as ever, an open overcoat revealing a button down shirt that fit perfectly. He smiled, as did I. We didn't need words; we walked into his apartment building and headed up. I reeked of alcohol, and I wondered what he thought of that. Did he even drink? Unsure and afraid to ask, I tried to keep it together.

Still drunk and happy beyond belief to be with him again, I tripped exiting the elevator. Luckily, he smiled, and we entered the apartment quietly. Sitting down on the couch that hours ago had been his bed, we chatted for a while. He didn't talk much, and I asked him why he was such a closed book. He said he wasn't, that he was just listening to me. I know I was rambling, as per the usual, about Rimbaud and his poetry and my annual visits to his grave. I remember bits and pieces of what I told him, but to be honest, all I wanted to do was feel his lips on mine.

We chatted for a long time, and somewhere in between, he opened up his kitchen cabinet, which revealed several bottles of wine. Happy to see that he wouldn't have disapproved of my drinking, I agreed to drink with him. He opened up a Chinon, poured us both glasses, and sat back down. As the evening went on, past the sunset and into the black of night, I felt so much happiness, I could have cried. He made me feel at home; I could be myself completely, and I was in a space free of judgment and hate.

I suggested laying down so we could be more comfortable, and he complied by stretching out the sofa-bed. His muscles flexed under his shirt as he lifted the bed, and my heart filled with desires I hadn't felt in months. We laid down with our wine still in our hands and sipped while we continued our conversation. I didn't learn much about him, but I did learn his family lived in Switzerland and that he usually spent his winter and summer breaks with them. He had thought often about moving, and passionately detested Paris' metro system.

He was a man of science and data. He liked patterns, found them everywhere, and absolutely adored finance and statistics. There was a beauty in science and being able to explain patterns, he said, and I remember mentioning there were some patterns even science couldn't explain. At this, we both realized I was talking about us, and he smiled and nodded in agreement. Somewhere in the very early hours of the morning, as sleepiness reared its head, he offered me his bed so I could be comfortable.

I stood up and held out my hand so that he could come with me. I didn't want to sleep alone, especially not with him in the next room. Luckily, he took my hand, and we laid down on the bed in our day clothes. I can't remember when we finally fell asleep, but I remember surrendering to the comfort of being with him. I woke up to chills at some point. The storm had persisted, and his apartment was frigid. He stirred and tried getting up, but I felt like I would freeze if he left me. I pulled him closer to me, and he put his arms around me.

As his body heat warmed me, I let out a sigh of relief. My yearning for him had taken hold of me, and I wanted to be his more than I've wanted anything in my life. I turned around to face him and looked into his eyes. I thanked him, and when he nodded, his chin hit my lips. The next instant, all of the passion I had been clinging to so desperately since I had met him came pouring out. We did this for hours, our bodies in perfect sync and our hearts beating furiously against our chests. He ran his hands against my back, which fueled the heat within me further. He pulled me into him, and we continued this way for several hours. He stopped every so often, complimenting my beauty, and I wondered if it was more for his benefit than mine. I wanted him with every fiber of my being, yet, I could tell he was holding back. Not wanting to push him for fear of losing the passion we were already sharing, I didn't insist. We fell asleep again, and when I woke up, he was already out of bed.

CHAPTER TWO

I lay in bed for some time, realizing what I had done. Eric and I may have been fighting, but we were still very much together. I would have to go home and confess to him that I had fallen for someone else and that things had happened between us. I would have to end it, and I would have to tell my family. I was sure they would judge me and blame me for the failure of our relationship, but I didn't feel remorse. Instead, my heart fluttered in excitement and reveled in the beautiful night I had spent in Guillaume's arms.

Feeling the need to spend every moment I could with him, I walked into the living room. He had prepared coffees and breakfast for us, and he walked over with the coffees as soon as I sat down on the sofa-bed where we had laid only hours before. I sipped my coffee and noticed Guillaume was lost in thought. He suddenly asked me if I would be ending things with my fiancé. I told him his name was Eric, which I regret doing. I'm sure Guillaume didn't care. I told him what had transpired the night before, and he nodded in understanding.

Not fully awake or sure how to approach the conversation, I told Guillaume I wasn't even sure Eric would be home. I didn't know what else to say, because I honestly didn't know which course of action would be best given what had just transpired. I could tell Guillaume wasn't happy with my answer, and as he grabbed my empty mug and took it back to the kitchen, I was overcome with a desire to end things with Eric as soon as I saw him.

In a hurry to do so and come back to Guillaume, I put on my shoes and grabbed my bag. He came with me until the metro stop, where we said our second formal goodbye. He seemed sad and broken, and as much as I wanted to tell him I was going to end it, it seemed unnatural and forced. I decided to say nothing instead; I would surely come back and tell him as soon as it was done. We would kiss again and again, and we would finally be able to explore the depth of our emotions to the fullest.

CHAPTER THREE

I stopped for a moment outside my apartment, preparing myself mentally for the conversation I needed to have. I walked into an empty apartment, with a note from Eric saying he had gone to see a movie and would be back in a few hours. I washed my face, brushed my teeth and headed into the shower. As much as I wanted to treasure the scent of Guillaume on me, I knew it would only add fuel to the fire that had been kindling.

Speaking of fires, I started one and sat there reading while the storm continued brewing outside. Minutes felt like decades, and after what seemed like an eternity, I heard the key turn in the lock. Eric walked in, and when he saw me, tears filled his eyes. He apologized, saying that he didn't know what had gotten into him, that he loved me more than I could understand, and that he had spent the evening talking to his mom, who had scolded him for treating me the way he had been.

He kneeled in front of me, teary-eyed and solemn, and asked me for one last chance. Torn between my guilt and my nostalgia, I simply nodded. I still don't know why I did it; just hours before, I knew that I wanted to end it and that nothing would deter me from doing so. Now, with his pleading and sorrow, I felt powerless. Eric kissed me softly, and as tears flooded my eyes, we hugged for some time. As for the conversations I needed to have with both of the men in my life, I decided to cross those bridges when I got there.

CHAPTER FOUR

With our plans to visit the family shredded to pieces because of our constant quarreling, we decided to spend a quiet Christmas at home. We exchanged the presents we had bought each other a month ago. He had bought me a beautiful Tiffany necklace with our names engraved on one of the hearts, and I had bought him a fancy shaving set and a couple of new ties for his upcoming interviews.

In the afternoon, he pulled me to the bed and kissed me sweetly. As I put my arms around him, my mind went back to Guillaume and the night before. I felt horrible and my guilt ate me as Eric caressed and kissed my entire body. We gave ourselves to each other, and at the end I could no longer hold back my tears. Bewildered and worried, he asked me what was wrong.

I told Eric that I needed to confess something. He stared at me, confused, and I shamefully admitted that I had spent the night with Guillaume. He said nothing at all, and with a stone-cold expression, he gathered a few belongings and left the apartment. I sat there, crying for a long time. I finally mustered the strength to leave the apartment and take a walk around the cemetery. Hopefully, there, I would find some solace and peace.

After a long walk and some thinking, I was certain Eric would never take me back. I was confused by my emotions. While I had wanted this to end, and I had hoped that I could run to Guillaume, I felt so much agony in losing Eric the way I had. I suppose I had wanted to stay with him after all. And if so, Guillaume had been nothing more than a whim of the heart in the absence of the Eric I knew and loved. Still torn and in a world of pain, I decided to go home.

Eric had come back and picked up all of his belongings in the few hours I had been gone. The apartment looked empty, cold, dead. All of his touches, from some of the artwork to the books he loved so much were now gone. I felt like I had walked into someone else's apartment, and it no longer felt like a home. I fell to my knees with the door still open, and with my palms covering my face, I sobbed endlessly.

The next few days were spent in much the same way. I didn't leave the house, I barely ate and cried constantly. Everything here reminded me of Eric, and the more he was gone, the more I missed him. I wanted to see him. I tried calling, texting, even emailing him, all to no avail. My calls were sent to voicemail almost immediately, and he never responded to a message or email. I felt hopeless, and in utter despair, reached out to his family to see if they had heard from him.

They denied knowing where he was, as did most of his friends. As I crossed off the list of people who might know where he was, I called the last friend, and from the way he dodged directly answering my questions, I was sure he knew Eric's whereabouts. I begged him to let Eric know how sorry I was and how much my life was incomplete without him. I wanted nothing more than for him to return my call or even see me so we could talk things out and work through them. He was my life, I said, and I couldn't imagine going on without him.

When New Year's Eve rolled around, I still hadn't heard from Eric. I wandered about the cemetery daily, broken-hearted and lifeless. As I planned to spend New Year's alone, I walked back to my empty and desolate apartment. I entered my apartment, and to my utter surprise, Eric was seated on the dining table, staring out the window. I could tell that he had been crying, and as I walked slowly towards him, he looked at me.

His first question was why. I explained that I had drank myself silly after our fight, and that he was the only one of my friends who was available. I had lied; I didn't want to hurt Eric more by saying that my heart had led me to Guillaume. He asked me if we had made love, and I repeatedly assured him we had not. Both of us cried, and after a long, painful talk, he said that he would come back, but only if I vowed to never see him again.

My heart was ripped from me once again. In all this time thinking about how I could get Eric back, I hadn't thought about what it would be like to say goodbye to Guillaume. It would be easy to do during vacation, but knowing we spent five out of seven days in the same building was a different story entirely. What if I ran into him? Would I have the willpower to stay away from him? Could I really promise Eric that the next time he and I fought I wouldn't find my way back to Guillaume?

It didn't matter if I could do it or not, I had to try. For the sake of Eric, for everything we had been through, and for his forgiveness, I owed him that much. If this was the only way I could keep him in my life, I would have to forget about the most memorable night of my existence and hopes of a meant-to-be romance that most people had only dreamed of their entire lives. I made the promise while tears ran uncontrollably down my face. Eric wiped them away and kissed me as I continued to apologize for my indiscretions.

As the new year brought promises of a happy relationship, I prepared for my teaching retreat in Angers the following week. Every year, to hone my teaching skills I went to the same retreat. With plenty of sessions hosted by renowned professors in the Humanities (and other schools of thought), I discovered new ways of improving my students' success. Eric seemed a changed man; I suppose the thought of losing me to someone else had shifted something within him. He had had multiple interviews, and a few of them seemed very promising.

That Thursday evening, as I finished the last of my packing, Eric walked in with fresh flowers and a huge smile on his face. He told me he had finally done it; he had gotten a job at a bank with a good salary and benefits. He lifted me up and swung me around in delight, and we laughed and celebrated with some wine. The next morning, I headed out early to catch my train to Angers.

CHAPTER FIVE

Given I would have an hour and a half of leisure time on the train, I picked one of my favorites books, *Paris est une Fête*, by Hemingway. I had read it many times before. Hemingway had been accurate in describing Paris as a moveable feast that never really left you no matter where life led you. This, in particular, had always appealed to me at the start of a new journey; it had become a tradition for me. With the horrible parts of the past year behind us and Eric's new job, I felt life had finally settled down, and a new chapter had begun.

A few minutes in, I froze. I looked up to find Guillaume walk into my compartment. I had never thought about the possibility that he would be there. My mind went into an immediate panic, and I wondered what I would tell Eric. I didn't think I should mention that Guillaume was there because if I did, I was sure I'd be expected to pack up and come back. As I struggled with the possibilities, I saw Guillaume glance at my left hand ring finger, and with a courteous smile, settle into the seat facing mine.

The universe sure has a way of testing you. It was bad enough that I would see him all weekend, but to sit in front of him for an hour and a half was a true test of my will. I pretended to read but I retained nothing. I would steal glances when he wasn't looking, though a few times, he caught me staring. When he fell asleep for about twenty minutes, I allowed myself to gaze freely, as much as I hated myself for doing so. The memories of our last night together flooded my mind and brought back the desire I had repressed for him.

When we finally reached Angers, I headed out to find a taxi. Recognizing a few coworkers, I quickly hurried to join them so that I wouldn't be stuck in one with Guillaume. We reached our hotel and checked in. Finally, in the privacy of my room, I allowed my emotions to sweep over me and cried for at least an hour. Everything I had tried to forget had come rushing back, and if it's even possible, I felt my heart ache. I fell asleep for a few hours, and when I finally awoke, it was nearly dinner time.

I headed down for the opening dinner and, luckily, had been placed at a table on the opposite end of Guillaume's. After dinner, I headed straight back up to my room instead of joining our group at the hotel bar. If I was to make it through this weekend, I needed to stay as far away from him as possible, even if that meant I would stay in my room during any free time we had.

I called Eric and filled him in on the uneventful day. I promised him I would try and see his family while I was here, though it may be difficult given I had three full days of lectures ahead of me. Ever so understanding, he told me not to worry, and that we would go see them together another time. I told him I loved him and meant it, and he returned the sentiment. When I hung up, I heard a soft knock on the door. I opened it up to find my coworkers, who hurried me in to grab my things so we could grab a drink downstairs. I insisted I wanted to get a good night's rest, but they weren't having it. When they wanted, they could be quite convincing. Begrudgingly, I grabbed my purse and room key and headed down to the lobby bar. After the first drink, they wanted to go to the nearest nightclub, a popular place called Mid'Star.

Reiterating that tomorrow would be a long day with an early start, I insisted I head back to my room. They dragged me out with them, and before I knew it, we were in a taxi headed to the nightclub. I hated nightclubs as it was, but more so given the fact that all I wanted was to be miserable and alone. After paying a cover charge, we entered the packed club and headed to the bar. Annoyed and tired, I decided I would need a drink to take the edge off. I ordered a gin and tonic, and as I turned around, I spilled it right onto Guillaume's shirt.

I apologized as I looked up at him, but he insisted he was fine. I grabbed some napkins from the bar and started to wipe the drink off of his shirt. He thanked me, but his tone told me I had overstepped. I handed him the napkins, and by the time this had transpired, I had lost sight of my friends. He asked if I had come alone, and I mentioned my coworkers were around. As we walked through the crowd, one of my coworkers grabbed us and pulled us onto the dance floor. We danced altogether for a while, and at one point she asked if he could take a picture of the two of us. She handed him her phone, and he took a few photos. She left us around fifteen minutes later to grab another drink.

The dance floor became more and more crowded, and the distance between Guillaume and I closed. We were less than a foot apart, and I did everything in my power to avoid his gaze. It had always been his eyes that had made me weak in the knees. The thought of a difficult but potential friendship crossed my mind when I wondered how I could keep him in my life, but before my thoughts were finished, he approached me to say something.

He told me he was happy for me, and that I had made the right decision in deciding to work on my relationship with Eric. Not fully knowing how I felt about what he was saying, I nodded. He continued on to tell me that he would like for us to be friends. Once again, I nodded, but I could feel tears rising in me. Said out loud, I realized the words I had been thinking moments ago weren't what I really wanted. I couldn't be his friend. I couldn't stand to be around him because every time I did, I lost all sense of self-control.

We continued dancing until someone bumped into me and I lost my balance. Guillaume pushed the guy aside and caught me, and with his hands on my waist and mine on his shoulders, we continued to dance. A second later, the man who had bumped into me seemed enraged by the fact that Guillaume had pushed him, and he came back, clearly to pick a fight. Guillaume put one hand on his shoulder, and as I ducked to prepare for a physical altercation, I heard him tell the young man to make peace, not war. No hard feelings, he said, and the young man, obviously disappointed to lose his shot at proving himself, walked away. I looked up at Guillaume, and if I hadn't been before, this was the moment I fell irrevocably in love with him. I had learned things about him, sure, but this side of him I hadn't seen.

He would have clearly won the fight, there was no denying it. Tall and muscular, Guillaume could have crushed the guy in a heartbeat. But he had chosen the mature route and even wished the guy a good night. His maturity and decency made him irresistible to me, and I felt more intoxicated than two drinks could have made me. Losing all of the control I had tried repeatedly to exert, I confessed to Guillaume that it was very hard to just be friends with him. In fact, I couldn't imagine a world where we could ever just be friends. I could tell he wanted to agree, but his will was stronger than mine. He told me that would be all we could ever be, which devastated me. I urged him to reconsider, but it seemed he had made up his mind. Caving in, I continued to dance with him, fighting back my tears.

We danced for over an hour. Seeing the sweat trickle down the sides of his head, I asked if he wanted to go get some water, but he refused every time I asked. His hands remained at my waist and mine at his shoulders, and with the increasing number of people on the dance floor, we were less than inches away. I pressed my lips onto his neck once, and despite the loud music, I swear I heard him sigh. Immediately after I did this, he took my hand and led me out of the dance floor to the bar. He bought us both bottles of water, and we stood there silently. He asked if I wanted to smoke and when I nodded, he took my hand and led me to the covered patio. We stood there quietly for some time until I finally brought back the topic of conversation on the dance floor. Here, again, he insisted that friendship was all that was in our cards, and that he couldn't be a homewrecker.

He went on to repeat I had made the right decision and would have to forget about whatever this was. I needed to focus on being a dutiful wife and someday, a good mother to Eric's children. I retaliated on every count, saying he didn't know anything about our relationship, and that while this was all easy for him to say, he wasn't the one living in it. Not ready to listen to a word I had to say, he raised his voice to tell me he had heard enough and wasn't going to change his mind. I could no longer hold back my tears, and I left him there, cigarette still dangling from his lips as I made my way through the club and out to the taxi stand. He followed me, and when I told him I needed to go, he offered to accompany me. I refused and headed back to the hotel alone. That night, I shed all the tears I had held in for so long. Tears for my trying engagement, tears for what I had felt with Guillaume, and tears for what would never be.

GUILLAUME

CHAPTER ONE

I waited for Hélène all day; she never came back. My heart sank deeper and deeper into the abyss that was my depression, but I had already known she wouldn't leave him. I had hoped she would fight for me, but here I was again, longing for a woman who hadn't want my heart as much as I had wanted hers. This was exactly why I had vowed off any romantic relationships; the disappointment burned within me, and for the first time in years, I shed tears for the loss of something I never really had.

The days passed by slowly. Christmas came and went, and as the weather grew colder, so did I. The barriers I had let down for Hélène closed back up, and before I knew it, I was drinking alone on New Year's Eve. I made only one resolution—the same one I had made years ago and forgotten—I would never again let a woman have me the way I had let Hélène. I would erase her from my memories, and I would do everything in my power to forget what we had shared.

I let myself remember, with excruciating pain and detail, every moment of every encounter we had ever had. I allowed myself to be absorbed by every emotion, and every time I reached our happiest moments, I reminded myself of what she had done to me. How she had danced around my question of the utmost vulnerability, how she had deserted me when I thought I had finally met someone who could give herself to me the way I had given myself to her.

The contrasting emotions weighed me down and filled me with an anger I hadn't felt in a long time. And then, apathy came. I went through this exercise as many times as was necessary so that I had drained out the positive and negative feelings towards her. All that was left then, was this unshakeable apathy. As I rang in the new year after a bottle and a half of champagne to myself, I felt nothing. I felt empty and devoid of any sentiment towards her.

CHAPTER TWO

As I packed my things for the annual teaching retreat, it crossed my mind that I may see her. I tested my durability yet again, and as I went through my aforementioned "cleansing" exercise, I realized the lack of sentiment had withstood the bitterness of the winter. Glad that I would not break my resolution, I gathered the last of my things and went to bed early. My dreams were as empty as I was, and I couldn't have been more relieved.

I saw her when I entered my car. As fate would have it, my seat was directly across from hers. I was polite, cordial and firm with her. I must confess, however, that on the inside, I felt rage and despair. I noticed she had on her engagement ring but decided to say nothing. What I really wanted to tell her was that she had used me to fuel her passions and left me when she had taken what she had wanted, but it would have gotten us nowhere. Clearly, she had already made her decision.

The old adage applied: if you don't have something nice to say, don't say anything at all. I sat down and opened up my newspaper. Diving right into the happenings of the day, I tried to forget she was in front of me. Fifteen minutes later, when the journey finally began, I found it harder to ignore her.

Every once in a while, I caught her staring as well. We locked eyes a few times I was secretly staring at her, but every time, she had gone back to scanning the room or reading her book and pretending it hadn't happened. For this much, at least, I was grateful.

I fell asleep for some time, and when I woke up, we were nearing the end of our journey. I was glad I had slept; sitting there awake had been torture. Every part of me wanted to hurt her and take her passionately all at once. We exited the train, and I was happy to see her hail a taxi with some other people. I grabbed my own, and in the solitude of my thoughts, I could tell that my strength, very present the night before, had started to say its goodbyes once more.

I smoked outside the hotel for some time, hoping that she would have checked in and headed up to her room by the time I was done. If I couldn't control how I felt around her, the least I could do is avoid run-ins. When I finally checked in, there was no sign of her in the lobby. To my relief, I headed up the elevator alone as well. Once in my room, I fell back onto the bed with my palms on my face, wondering how I would be able to get through the entire weekend. For a moment, I contemplated leaving, but in the interest of my long-term goals, I decided I would just have to deal with it.

Later that evening, I met some friends at the bar before dinner. I caught a glimpse of her exiting the elevator but turned away from her before she could see me. Resuming my conversation with some of the professors I had just met, I tried to erase her from my mind. As always, I was unsuccessful in doing so. I headed to the dinner table and was glad to know we had been placed on opposite ends of the room. I purposely chose a seat where my back faced hers in an attempt to eliminate any stolen glances or forced smiles.

CHAPTER THREE

A few of the professors had decided to head out to a nearby club after dinner. Agreeing to go in hopes it would take my mind off of Hélène, I got dressed and headed to the lobby to meet them an hour later. When we arrived, the club was still a bit empty, but it gave me enough time to take a couple of shots of whiskey and order a whiskey & ginger. The buzz kicked in fairly quickly, as did the throngs of people ready to dance the night away. I walked out to the smoking patio and took long drags of my Gauloises. After I had smoked three cigarettes in succession, I headed back to the bar to refill my drink. I stood in line, half buzzed and distracted by just how packed the club was getting.

I got my drink and turned around to make my way back outside, when I felt a cold sensation on my chest. Hélène was already apologizing profusely and had grabbed some napkins to wipe down my shirt. She had walked right into me drink-first and begun to wipe down my chest. She must have seen my discomfort at her touch, for she handed me the napkins. I continued to wipe down my shirt as we walked away. Buzzed off of my drinks and aggravated to semi-drunkenness by my deep inhalations, I started conversing with her. I asked her if she had come alone, and she informed me that her coworkers were there as well. A moment later, I felt a tug on my arm, and before I understood what was happening, her coworker, Hélène and I were on the dance floor.

We danced for some time, and I could sense the awkwardness that surrounded us. None of us said a word to one other, and I was glad when her coworker asked me to take photos of the two of them. I complied, happy to have something else to do besides think about how beautiful Hélène looked. Her coworker left us at some point thereafter, and as the crowds of people rushed to the dance floor, the gap between us grew smaller. I was absolutely petrified. I had done everything I could since I had been in Angers to avoid her, and now I was closer to her than I had ever imagined. I could feel my heart beat furiously, and my resolve rapidly desert me.

In an effort to compose myself, I told her how happy I was for her. She looked disappointed, but I knew I had to say it. As much as it broke my heart, as much as it was partly a lie, I knew that if I left a door open, we would end up back where we had been the last time, and my heart wouldn't recover if this happened again. I told her she had made the right decision in working on her relationship with Eric, and that we would be friends. Visibly upset, she didn't say anything but nodded quietly instead.

I was startled by a sudden movement and realized a young fellow had run into her in an effort to get past her. I pushed the guy aside and caught her just as her ankle was about to roll. She held onto my shoulders as I held onto her waist, and I was certain my heart was in my throat by this point. Our bodies were pressed together, and as I gathered myself, I saw flashes of our night together rush back with every emotion I had felt. I felt a hand on my shoulder, and the gentleman I had pushed aside had clearly taken my action to mean I wanted a fight. I put my hand on his shoulder, and calmly explained fighting wasn't the answer. In his youth and inebriation, I'm sure he would have loved nothing more than to prove he could win. And while I knew I could take him, there was no reason to start something when it all stemmed from a misunderstanding. As much as I trained my body for the worst of situations, my philosophy had always been that words could win wars that fists simply couldn't.

I looked back at her as she had steadied herself, and I saw something change in her eyes. I don't know why, but I knew that in this moment, she had fallen for me more deeply than she had anticipated, and in return, my heart was forever hers. I don't know for certain if that's how she felt, but the look she gave me broke every resolution I had ever made. I was hers. I felt connected with her thoughts and her soul, and in this I found tremendous beauty.

A wave of sadness and profound love hit me the very next instant, knowing full well that this would be the last time I would get to hold her like this. Whatever had changed within her, she was still very much engaged. And from our past encounters, I knew that was not likely to change. More so, I knew that I had to do the right thing. My principles were my foundation, and if I let this weaken me again, I would not be able to face myself. Knowing where her future was and should be headed, I kept her close to me, and surrendered only to my feeling of not wanting to let her go. I wouldn't have her for the rest of my days, but that night, in the club, I had her in my arms. And that would be enough.

She drew closer, and as I felt her warm breath on my ear, she told me it was hard to just be friends. She mentioned she couldn't imagine a world where we would just be friends. I wanted so desperately to agree, and with the same breath, I wanted to tell her how much she had hurt me, how much pain she had caused. I wanted to ask her why she hadn't fought for me and come back for me that day. Instead, all I could do was shake my head to disagree, and I ultimately saw her give up.

I had tried, for the last hour, to keep myself at bay. I was sweaty from my nervousness, I was parched, and yet I had stayed there because I knew I would never have this moment with her again. But when she pressed her lips against my neck, it took everything in me to not follow my heart and leave the world behind. I took her hand and moved us off of the dance floor to the bar. I ordered us waters and handed her a bottle. Needing a distraction, I asked if she cared for a smoke. She nodded, and in an effort to avoid being separated, I took her hand and led her outside.

As we pushed past the crowd, I thought back to the pain I had felt. I rationalized; it's what I did best. I reminded myself that not only had she cheated on her fiancé, she had used me and deserted me for him. I couldn't trust someone who had broken two hearts just to keep hers happy. I didn't have any guarantee that if we did this, if we decided to be together, that she would never do this to me again. After all, our great romance had started on the basis of lies. I felt terrible thinking these things of her, but I knew I had to deter myself somehow. My principles, yet again, mattered more to me.

We both smoked, and I hoped she had forgotten about our conversation. Alas, she brought it up again and reiterated her refusal of a friendship. Despite my whims to give in, I insisted friendship was all that was in our cards. I refused to be a homewrecker, and she had absolutely made the right decision. She needed to be a good wife. Someday, she would have to be a good mother to his children. Of course she wasn't happy, and she angrily expressed that I wasn't in her relationship and that it was easier said than done.

I lost my patience, and with a sternness that surprised me as much as her, let her know I had had enough. Tears filled her eyes, and she ran out of the smoking patio into the club. I dropped my cigarette and chased after her out to the taxi stand. I asked if she wanted company, but she refused, and so I watched her leave. The number of times an encounter with this woman had left my heart shattered in pieces astounded me, and I had no more strength left. I hailed a cab and headed back to the hotel. A few smokes in and certain I wouldn't run into her, I headed up to my room. I took a hot shower, trying to wash off her scent and more memories that would haunt me for a lifetime. Sleep eluded me most of the night, and when my eyes finally shut, I couldn't say.

CHAPTER FOUR

The next morning, I didn't see her when I got to breakfast. It was possible she had come down earlier, or that she had decided to skip breakfast altogether. Whatever the reason, I ate my breakfast in peace, grateful that my will would not be tested at least for the next hour. As I chatted with the professors at my table, I noticed a sudden change in my temperature. I was burning up, and not knowing why, decided to retire to my room for some rest before the lectures began.

The elevator door was about to close when I saw a hand reach for it. I helped, and as it opened up, I saw Hélène freeze. She told me she could take the next one, but I insisted. She walked in, and standing on the opposite end of the elevator, pressed the button for the third floor. We didn't say a word to each other. This time, however, it wasn't a comfortable silence. I noticed her eyes were swollen and red, and I hated myself for my cruelty towards her the night before. I wanted to apologize, but I knew it would only open up a can of worms. There was no way my will would withstand yet another battle between what I wanted more than anything in the world and what I needed to do.

As she exited the elevator, she didn't look back. I went up to the fifth floor, and back in my room, I fell asleep almost immediately. When I woke up, it was lunch time. I had missed the morning lectures. Still feeling a bit faint and warm, I headed down to the banquet hall I had left hours ago. As I found my table, I noticed Hélène seated at the table next to me. Once again, refusing to tempt myself, I sat with my back facing her. Almost immediately, I saw her pass me by with palms covering her face. She was headed to the elevator. A few moments later, she was gone.

I reminded myself that as much as it hurt to be this ruthless, I had to do it for both of us. She needed to be with him; she needed to give her relationship a real chance. And I needed to let her. With loving someone so much came the selfless desire to let them be happy. Not just in the moment, but for a lifetime. She clearly had history with this man and had loved him enough to forsake me once. That much love didn't disappear at a moment's notice, and I knew that if I caved, I would only have deprived her of the chance at a happy life with him.

She never came back down to eat. I saw her later that day, in one of the afternoon lectures, and she didn't so much as acknowledge my presence in the room. Despite being seated in the same row, she never once looked over, and I got a bitter taste of my own medicine. It broke my heart to be this close to her and yet eons apart, but I knew it was for the best. This way, I wouldn't impede her happiness, and she wouldn't someday regret leaving Eric for me. Whether this was my self-deprecating nature or more love than I've ever had for another human being, I don't know.

That evening, she was another no-show at dinner. When I turned in for the night, I tossed and turned for hours, wondering if she had eaten at all. I wandered back down to the bar in hopes of inquiring with one of her coworkers. Luck was in my favor; as I walked in, the coworker who had briefly joined us on the dance floor walked over to me. She asked if we had had a good time, and I nodded quietly. I asked her if she had seen Hélène, and when she said that she had not responded to any messages and had been absent most of the day, I asked if she knew her room number.

I must have sounded like a stalker. Bewildered and a bit reticent, she asked me why I wanted to know. I made up a lie about Hélène not feeling well last night and told her the truth about wanting to send some food to her room. She obliged at this point, and I found out she was in room 328. I called room service to order a grilled cheese— remembering she was vegetarian from the dinner we had had the night she had fallen—and asked them to send the food to her room but the bill to mine. An hour and a half later, I heard a knock on my door. With a mix of anxiety and hope, I opened the door, only to find the room serviceman at my door with the food. I explained to him that the food needed to go to 328. He advised he had tried, but that she had refused the food. I decided to go speak with her myself. I paid and tipped the serviceman, then pushed the tray into the elevator and headed to the third floor.

HÉLÈNE

CHAPTER ONE

The next morning, I had no desire to leave my room and face Guillaume. My head pounded from the thousands of tears I had shed the night before, and the sunlight streaming in through the sheer curtains only aggravated it. I popped two pain killers I had brought with me (I was still recovering from the residual pain from my fall) with a little water. I went in to take a shower, and as I shed my clothes, I could smell Guillaume on every part of me. My clothes, my hands, even my hair smelled of him.

I started to feel a bit better but not enough to see him, so I decided to go to the lobby bar and order breakfast there. I finished quickly and headed back to the room so I could sleep some more before lectures began. The elevator door was just about to close when I stuck my hand in to stop it. The longer I lingered in the lobby, the more chances I had of running into him. And with my swollen, puffy eyes, red as blood, I would be quite the sight.

A hand reached out to help open the elevator, and I was immensely thankful for a moment. That is, until I found myself face-to-face with Guillaume. Not wanting to be inches away from him, I politely declined, stating I could take the next one, but he insisted. I walked in and immediately placed myself on the opposite side. I pressed the button to get to the third floor and noticed he had pressed the fifth. Grateful we weren't on the same floor and wouldn't be stuck with small talk while walking to our rooms, I breathed a sigh of relief. When the elevator door opened, I walked out without a glance in his direction. In my room, tears flowed easily once again, and somewhere in a state of delusion and pain, I passed out.

I woke up an hour later, and already late to the first lecture, decided I would catch the second one. I walked out to the front of the hotel and stood smoking for some time. I reflected on the night before, on how distant, cold and mean he had been. I couldn't understand why he had yelled at me. Or why he had wanted nothing to do with me anymore. I could have sworn I had seen a glimpse of love in his eyes when he held me close, but maybe, sadly, I had imagined it all. And once again, Eric came to mind. I called him immediately, and when he didn't answer, I felt lonelier.

I walked into the next lecture, and I couldn't have told you what it was about or who was speaking. I felt like death and surely looked like it too. My mind was far away, trapped in thoughts of an uncertain and potentially unhappy, unfulfilled future. I didn't know how I would go back to my life in Paris, knowing Guillaume was always a stone's throw away. I didn't know how I would go home to Eric without breaking down again. As these thoughts inundated me, I had hardly noticed the lecture was finished and I was the only one left in the room.

I found my table at lunch. There was no sign of Guillaume just yet, and I was thankful. It was going to be a long, torturous few days, and the less I saw him the better I would surely feel. As soon as some measure of peace set in, I saw him walk in. I inhaled sharply as I realized he was headed to my table and finally exhaled when he stopped at the table next to mine. I knew he had seen me, but he chose the seat facing away from me. It was one thing to push off my advances, but to purposely sit facing away from me was simply unnecessary. I felt humiliated and ran out of the room with my hands covering my face.

A half an hour later, it was time for the afternoon lectures. In the time I had spent in my room, I had decided I had had enough. No more yearning, no more weakness. I would do what I had come here to do, which was to learn and grow. I would go home to Eric, who loved me. I would marry him, and we would live a happy life together. Guillaume's cruelty had done me a favor; it had made me hate him. And in this hate, I had found solace. In this hate, my love for him had dissolved. It was a tour de force for which I was grateful, and it gave me the courage to charge back downstairs. No seating arrangement or elevator ride would discourage me; two could play this game. I hadn't been this cold in a long time, but if this is what he had wanted, this is what he would get.

We both ended up in the same lecture. I made no attempt to even glance in his direction. My aura spewed hatred, and I sat as still as a statue, focused on every word of the lecture. I didn't once allow my mind to wander, and as soon as the lecture was done, I headed to my room. I would order some food when I felt like it, but I would not be humiliated again. I tried Eric again, but once again my call went to voicemail. I sent him a text saying I missed and loved him, and to call me as soon as he got the message. I laid on the bed, devoid of any emotions. Every moment of the day went through my head and I cursed myself for having been so weak. I wished more than anything that I could have been like my mother or my sister. No one dared to mess with them; they were bold, courageous women and they never let anyone walk all over them.

A couple of hours later, I saw Eric's name light up my phone. Thankful for the distraction, I picked up, only to hear his voice in the distance, and some woman laughing closer to the phone. I thought I had misread the name on my phone, but I checked again, and it was definitely Eric. I pressed my ear to the receiver and realized he didn't seem to know I was on the other end. I thought I heard him mention my name. Before I knew it, the passion between them had intensified. With the reflexes of a cat, I slammed my phone shut, deafened by the silence that now surrounded me. I sat there and stared blankly for a long time. Tears had, by now, become my constant companion, and the thought that I had lost two men I loved in the same twenty-four hour span broke my spirit.

I grabbed the wine bottle I had brought with me for the last night, opened it and started chugging. Whatever this pain was, I wanted to dull it as quickly as possible. Being conscious was my biggest hindrance in doing so, and so I drank. I had finished half the bottle when I heard a knock on my door. Afraid my coworkers had come to take me out again, and with no will left to hide my pain, I opened the door in tears. To my surprise, t was room service. I was told a gentleman on the fifth floor had especially requested the food to be brought to me. Knowing full well who this gentleman was, I thanked the hotel staff member and kindly refused. Shutting the door behind me before he could retort, I went back to drinking. Not long after, I heard another knock. Thinking about the relentlessness of the hotel staff and ready to tell them I was not in the mood, I opened the door to find Guillaume standing there. He certainly didn't look happy with me, and I couldn't have cared less.

CHAPTER TWO

Without waiting for an invitation, Guillaume walked in and began pacing the room. I tried shutting the door behind me but failed the first time and stumbled back to close it. He noticed the half drank bottle on the nightstand and waved it in my face. He asked if I had eaten anything at all, and I shook my head in denial. He asked me why I was doing this to myself, and while I should have felt loved or cared for, all I could feel was rage. I asked him why he cared; I asked him why it mattered if I ate or starved myself, or if I existed at all.

He seemed shocked at my honesty, and with a change in both tone and expression, asked me what was wrong. A part of me wanted to tell him what I had just heard, to seek comfort in him, but the other part of me was still fuming from the utter humiliation I had suffered at the hands of these two men. I asked him again why he cared, to which he just shook his head. Of course he cared, he stated matter-of-factly, and asked me to stop drinking. He grew serious again and told me I needed to eat the food he had brought with him. He headed to the door, and holding it open with one leg, pulled in the room service cart.

I continued to refuse to eat, and he switched from scolding to pleading. He was worried about me, he said, and wanted to ensure that I was taking care of myself. He did care about me and always would. With every ounce of my being, I fought the desire to run into his arms and tell him what had happened. In defiance, as was always my strong suit, I picked up the bottle and started violently chugging my wine.

He tried to grab the bottle from me, and when he finally succeeded, I fell onto the floor on my knees, wailing. If I could have seen his face amidst my tears, I would have imagined a look of sheer disbelief or horror. Or both. I looked no different than a child throwing a temper tantrum. Without judgment and with the utmost tenderness, he lifted me to my feet and sat me down on the edge of the bed. With his firm hands, he lifted my chin so I would face him, his palms covering my cheeks and thumbs wiping my tears. Tears were still running down my cheeks incessantly, and I sobbed this way for a long time. He pulled me into his chest, and by the time I was done crying, his shirt was soaked.

I could tell he knew something had gone horribly wrong but didn't dare ask again. After the crying had stopped and an uncomfortable silence had swept the room, I felt the hunger that had started devouring me. I told him I would like to eat, and without asking, he brought the food over and started to hand feed me. I tried to smile as I looked in his eyes, at his furrowed brow, still filled with worry. I tried to be reassuring; I told him I would be fine. I thanked him for his kindness, for his lack of judgment, and for my sheer luck that he was there when I needed someone the most. In what I imagine to be his efforts to control himself, he responded with a generic "that's what friends are for" and smiled. I hated his response; I wanted and needed more, but I think I finally understood. He was being strong for both of us, not just for himself. With this wave of comprehension, I realized I would have to let him go. I had struggled with it all day, but I had had Eric. When I left Guillaume, he had no one.

If he had waited for my return, I could only imagine how crushed and humiliated he had felt. And there he was, comforting me in my darkest hour. Even if he didn't know what was happening, he had put everything aside to hold me. If it was anything like the pain I had felt when I knew we couldn't be anything more than friends, it must have been killing him too. I stared at him while I ate, and behind the tough exterior, I caught a glimpse of his pain.

I decided to share what I had just heard, and his face fell as much as mine had some time ago. He expressed how sorry he was for what I was going through and asked if he could do anything. I thanked him for everything he had already done. After all, he had not only been there for me as I broke down, he had also stayed to comfort and feed me. I wanted to ask him to stay, but I knew it wouldn't be fair to him. After all, I had only ever appeared to need him when Eric wasn't there for me. I couldn't ask him to do it again.

When at last I had finished my meal, he said he would take the cart down and be back in a few minutes. I figured this was his way of politely taking his leave, and I didn't stop him. I was surprised when he returned some time later, a wine bottle in each hand. He sat down next to me on the edge of the bed, and as he opened one of the bottles, I learned more about the man I have never stopped loving since the day I laid eyes on him.

CHAPTER THREE

I got up to find some glasses. Still drunk from half a bottle of wine on an empty stomach, I tumbled into Guillaume. In an effort to catch me, he let the wine opener fall to the ground, and when I tried to walk I realized the sharp end had fallen on my big toe and cut it open. He made a joke about me being a walking liability, and we laughed. I told him I had a first-aid kit and went to go grab it from my suitcase. Once again he sat there, carefully cleansing my cut and applying a bandage on my foot. His warm hands touched my cold foot, and it sent shivers up the length and breadth of my entire body. Snapping back to reality, I hobbled over and grabbed the glasses on the desk. He filled both glasses generously, and we moved from the edge of the bed to the floor, with our backs resting against the twin-sized frame. He asked me how I was doing, and I shrugged. I made a joke about karma, and he sighed. With an urge I could not repress, I told him how sorry I was that I didn't come back that day.

It was the first honest conversation we had had since. Amidst our fears and iron wills, neither of us had been truthful with the other. That night, we let it all out. He told me he had hoped I would come back but on some level, he had already accepted the fact that I belonged to someone else. Good things didn't happen to him, he had said, and whenever they did, there was a price to pay. It made me sad to think that this man, this wonderful, loving man had never held on to a single good thing in his life. He talked of his tense family dynamic and his past love who had broken him. He had turned cold and had vowed never to let anyone else in the way he had let her. I had changed that, and he had to change it back once I had made my decision.

I say honest because we did share how we felt. What we didn't share was the repression of the desires that still gnawed at us. I knew without a doubt we wanted to be together. I knew without a doubt he loved me as much and as deeply as I loved him. What we shared instead, however, was what we had done to each other. The words he shared that night have never left me. Sometimes, I still find myself repeating them. Tears always come quickly, and they are the only reminders I have left of Guillaume:

"Hélène," he said as he sighed, "I feel you when you're in the room, my heart sinks to the depths of my body when I say your name. We are inextricably and irrevocably linked in this web of possibilities, and yet, all we've ever caused each other is pain. I realized fairly early on that we had the power to either completely fulfill one another, or completely destroy one another. We have done nothing but the latter. You want to change the world through education. I want to change the world through science. Our goals are larger than this, than us. We will only stand in the way of them if we pursue this."

After pausing for a moment to hide the break in his voice, he said, "I want us to have a real chance to fulfill our dreams. If the fates bring us back to each other, I won't fight it. But for now, we need to go our separate ways and be the persons we have strived for so long to be. And if the day comes when you are brought back to me or I to you, there will be no force strong enough to keep us apart. This much, I promise you. I have loved you since the day I met you, even if I have denied it or tried to rationalize it. And I'm sure I'll love you for several lifetimes. But I would hate myself if I stood in the way of us realizing our full potential as individuals and take away from the world what we have to offer on account of our selfish desires. So please, don't take this as a sign of my hatred or reproach for you. Take this as my love for us, as my desire to see you grow and flourish, and to see myself do the same."

His eloquence astonished me. So far, he had always seemed to me to be a man of few words. He had never opened up to this extent, and in this one weekend, I had found in him the man I had spent a lifetime seeking. I cried with the entire weight of my soul, and as I did, I saw tears in his eyes as well. As much as I hated this separation, I knew he was right. The closer we got, the farther away our dreams would go. I didn't want to stand in his way to greatness, and I was thankful he valued my dreams. Agreeing to stay friends, we continued drinking.

When I woke up the next morning, he was gone. The loneliness enveloped me, and his words lingered in my head. I feared the universe may never bring us back together. Maybe our chance encounters had run their due course, and if so, we were destined to stay apart. This may have been the only real chance we had had, and like everything else, this too was gone. Hungover and devastated at the possibility we would never be together, never get to explore what might have been, my head felt ready to explode. I took two painkillers with an entire bottle of water. I finally forced myself to shower and head down for breakfast, but through all of it, I grieved for the loss of the love I would possibly never have.

GUILLAUME

CHAPTER ONE

I rushed to her floor with the food. She was being unnecessarily dramatic. It was one thing to feel broken; I felt broken in my own way, but another completely to starve oneself and blow things out of proportion. She knew I had noticed she had missed breakfast, lunch and now dinner, and so there was no surprise that between the tight schedule of our lectures which I assume she had attended, there was no time left to eat.

Yes, I cared about her. Yes, I loved her. But the more time I spent with her, the more I realized I didn't quite know the real Hélène. It was likely this was the rational part of my brain saying I needed to distance myself because of all the pain I had suffered at her hands. Or maybe there was really something to this feeling of uncertainty. Either way, however much I may have hated her childish behavior, I wasn't heartless.

I knocked on her door. She opened it red-eyed and unfocused. I already knew she was drunk when I barged in. I paced the room so I could figure out how to best reason with someone who was so intoxicated they could barely shut the door. It wasn't long before I noticed the half-empty bottle. There was no used glass in sight.

I held the bottle up to her face, mostly so she wouldn't try and hide the fact that she was drunk. I asked her if she had bothered to eat anything, but I already knew the answer to my question. When she answered, I was disappointed to find she had played into all of my assumptions about her. There was the dramatic questioning of why I cared if she ate, if it mattered whether she ate or starved, or if she existed at all.

I kept my composure; clearly, there was something that had bothered her to this point, and I tried not to assume it was related to me, to us. I asked her what was wrong. She asked me again why I cared, and I shook my head in disappointment. The woman whom only last night I had hoped to hold on to as long as I could, had turned into this pitiful, dramatic person; one whom I found it hard to respect. Despite my annoyance, I found the strength to tell her I cared. For all we had been through, whether or not it mattered now, I had cared for her. That had not changed. As stoic as I could be, and as distant as I had forced myself to be, I couldn't deny how important she was to me.

I asked her to stop drinking and to eat something. I headed to the door and pushed in the food cart. I knew my tone wasn't helping, and in an effort to get her through the night without being sick, I begged her to eat. My pleading didn't help either; in return, she grabbed the remaining wine and started chugging. I reached my breaking point, grabbed the bottle from her hands and pulled as hard as I could. To my amusement, she pulled back. This is the first time I had seen her be adamant about anything, and a part of me was charmed. Eventually, I got a hold of the bottle.

I couldn't believe my eyes and ears when she fell to the ground and emitted a high-pitched yelping sound. When I finally processed the ridiculousness of her reaction, I was certain something had gone terribly wrong. When she had been sober, she had been at her most graceful, and this was a side of her I had never imagined I would see. With her episode also came the understanding that she couldn't have wished for anyone to see her this way either, least of all me.

Snapping out of my thoughts, I lifted her to her feet. I helped her settle down at the edge of the bed and held up her face, gently wiping away her tears. As shocked as I was by this whole ordeal, I could tell something had deeply disturbed her. Moreover, I had promised her a friendship, and a good friend would not desert another in their time of need. I pulled her into me, and as her tears left their mark on my shirt, a part of me felt her pain.

After a while, she lifted her head and it seemed the tears had finally run their due course. A silence followed, somewhat uncomfortable but entirely expected. She finally spoke to me, and I was happy to hear that she was ready to eat. I fed her myself, ensuring she felt comforted. I may not have loved her with the same intensity I had until tonight, but there was a part of me that still felt very connected to her. I wanted to be there and ensure she didn't feel deserted.

She must have sensed my discomfort because she tried assuring me she would be OK. Only half-smiling, and forcibly so, she thanked me for my kindness, for my lack of judgment and expressed how grateful she was I was there. I told her that's what friends were for, and she gave me an inquisitive look. Silence followed, and I wondered what she was thinking about until she finally explained why she had been so emotional.

Apparently, while Eric was with another woman, he had accidentally dialed Hélène. She had heard everything. My heart felt heavy for her. I could relate; I knew how it felt to know someone you loved so deeply had given their body and soul to another. My heart relapsed a bit, and I felt the pain I had felt only days ago when I realized she had chosen him over me.

I told her how sorry I was. Selfishly, the heartfelt apology stemmed from the feeling I had experienced, more so than from how I imagined she must feel. She thanked me for all I had done for her as she continued eating. When she finished her meal, I decided I wouldn't desert her, and since I was already here, I would continue to keep her company. For once, I wasn't focused on the intensity of the love I felt for her. It wasn't the time for that; it was for compassion and empathy. Or maybe it was sympathy. I'm not sure I would have been able to relate to what she was going through if she hadn't done the same to me. To me, that's what differentiates sympathy and empathy. You don't need to be in someone's shoes to be empathetic. You simply need to feel for them, be kind and above all, be patient. The difference didn't matter anyway; I had decided to be sympathetic, I suppose, and so I decided I would return the food cart and grab some wine. After all, misery does love alcohol.

I let her know I would be back soon and left the room. I headed down to the lobby to return the food cart and started to have second thoughts. I wanted to ensure my return didn't make any promises on my behalf. I didn't want her to think anything would happen between us, or that we would fall back into the desire that had overcome us two weeks ago. I also wondered if my return would imply I would be there when she left Eric, waiting for her to be mine. Two weeks ago, this is exactly what I had wanted. But now, after she had chosen him over me, I couldn't imagine going through the cycle again. Without giving it another thought, I grabbed a couple of bottles of wine. I could be an empath, I could even be a good friend, but I couldn't be a liar. I told her I would be back, and I kept my promise. I went back to her room, and I could tell by the surprised expression on her face that she hadn't expected me to come back.

CHAPTER TWO

I'm sure she knew how much I had disapproved chugging from the bottle because she got up to find some glasses. Still drunk, she ran into me and knocked the wine opener out of my hand as she got up. It was a few minutes before I noticed that the sharp end had landed on her left foot. In an effort to divert her attention from the pain, I made a joke about her inability to walk and how she should be monitored at all times. Luckily, she laughed. She went to grab her first aid kit. Knowing she was too drunk to do anything, I played the role of nurse yet again. The nostalgia of our first night together swept me as I cleaned and dressed her wound, but my bruised ego kept me sane. I washed the memory from my mind almost immediately, and I focused on the task at hand so that there would be no infection the next day.

She grabbed two glasses from the desk, which I poured generously to ensure I could resist the urge to leave. I sat down on the floor with my back against the bed, mainly to resist temptation, and she followed. Not really sure what to say after what she had shared, I asked her how she was doing. She shrugged in response. She made some strange joke about karma. My mind wandered to the night she didn't return, and how foolish I had been to think that a woman who had everything—the perfect job, a man who loved her, a wedding only a few months away—would have given all of that up for a stranger she barely knew. As if she could read my thoughts, she apologized for not having returned that day.

I felt like I owed her something. Some sort of peace, some sort of explanation; just something to make her feel like she hadn't just lost everything she had hoped for her entire life. To be clear, it's not that I didn't love her or hope that things had worked out. The connection I had with her was honestly something I had never experienced with anyone else. But my past, my principles and the vows I had made to myself (and had already broken) reminded me I couldn't pursue this. For once, the words people never believe at the end of a relationship were true: it wasn't her, it was me.

I confessed I knew whenever she was around, how heavy I felt when I said her name. In an effort to assuage her spirit, I also told her that it wasn't our time. That as much as I loved her, we had bigger things to do. I remembered how much she cared about her students, how much she put into it so they could pave the way for a better future. I reminded her of her goals, and I shared mine. I told her that if somehow fate decided we should meet again, I wouldn't fight it. But for now, our best hope for any sort of future was to fulfill our personal destinies and be the best versions of ourselves.

As true as every word was, I hadn't been completely honest. The events that had followed our passionate night together had left me with resentment and bitterness. I knew I would avoid any path that led to her. I knew this would be my last teaching retreat. I also knew I had already applied to universities abroad, and that my chances of leaving were high. I knew that part of me was tempting fate; that part of me wanted to see if something would bring me back to her. And I knew that the likelihood of this happening was very low. She loved Paris; she always had and always would. If I moved to Switzerland or the Netherlands, our paths would never cross again.

In promising her the hand of fate, I had promised her nothing. Strangely, I felt free. Of her, of this curse, of the hold she had on me, and of everything I had experienced in the past year. The uneasiness that had stayed with me since the first day I had met her suddenly started its dissent. The pain I had tried so hard to overcome now seemed insignificant. Whatever this was, it had given me a peace I had longed for since I met her, and hopefully it was one that would last me a lifetime.

As luck would have it, she understood. She cried for a long time. I cried with her, not for the loss of her, but for the loss of what we would never be. The loss I mourned for was the loss of a connection I had never before had with anyone else, and possibly would never have with anyone else. The tears I shed were not for her, Hélène, but for the hope of all-consuming love, which now seemed nothing more than a fading memory. Like everything else I had ever yearned for in life, I would find no happy ending.

We agreed to stay friends, though I knew this was also a farce. I could never be friends with her. In the one year I had known this woman, I had seen her selfishness, I had seen her infidelity, and I had seen her rage. I had also seen her core, her passion and her love. No matter which of the two sides I chose to focus on, it would be impossible to be around her. Finally, given how physically and emotionally drawn we were to each other, friendship was simply not an option. When she finally fell asleep, I lifted her and laid her on the bed. I kissed her forehead gently, knowing this would be the last time I would ever be this close to her. I wished her the best, and as she stirred, I turned off the lights and left the room.

CHAPTER THREE

After only one more lecture in her presence, and two days of insight from renowned professionals, we headed home. I purposely missed my train and decided to spend an extra day in Angers. I explored the old castle and enjoyed a few bottles of the infamous Layon wine. I was grateful for the alone time. Introverted and extremely exhausted from the emotional toll this weekend had taken on me, I had welcomed the self-indulgence.

The next day, I took the first train home. I checked the mail as soon as I got home and found an employment offer from the University of Amsterdam. I had interviewed with them before leaving for Angers, and given my mood at the time, was sure I had failed miserably. The pleasant surprise reassured me, and as I got on the phone with my family to inform them, I made plans to leave the past year behind me.

A sorting of affairs was in order. I had purchased my apartment, so the first thing I needed to do was find someone to rent it for at least a year. Uncertain about my acclamation to a new country, I wanted to ensure I didn't have someone sign a five-year lease, only to be homeless should I return sooner than expected. I listed ads online and in the local university newsletters, hoping to find a student who needed a reasonably-priced apartment in Paris. As I waited to hear back, I searched for apartments in Amsterdam, and thanks to my hefty savings, settled on a cozy loft in the city centre.

The prospect of a new beginning had a marvelous effect on me. I would only have one more semester before I could move on with my life, and I had already planned to switch my schedule to night classes (which were less desirable) so as to avoid any potential contact with Hélène.

The university happily accepted my proposal, and so every day, I got to campus in the late afternoon and most days, didn't leave until after nine in the evening. A heavy snowstorm took over Paris for a few weeks in late February. I counted down exactly three and a half months until I would be free of this city, and the excitement only grew. Luck must have been on my side, since not once in the remaining months did I see Hélène. No goosebumps, no tumble down the stairs, not even a staff meeting encounter. I wasn't sure if she was even teaching there anymore, but whatever the reason was, I was grateful.

HÉLÈNE

CHAPTER ONE

I saw Guillaume only once after that night. We had a lecture together the next day, and as we had decided, I kept my distance. No stolen glances, no silent communication. I sat on the opposite end of the room, as out of sight as I possibly could have been. I felt empty, but I reminded myself of his words, and they gave me strength. I had already messaged Eric to be gone by the time I returned, and for once I was grateful he hadn't had a job for months. I knew there was no way he could have kept the apartment. With his first paycheck about a month away, he would not have been able to pay the bills.

I took the train home Monday evening as scheduled, and I had a feeling Guillaume wouldn't be on it. With the promise he had made me, I knew he would avoid any commonplace encounter to the best of his ability. Shared spaces were off limits, of course. La Sorbonne, the train back to Paris, the retreat; all of these would have nothing to do with fate and everything to do with our shared environment. When I finally got home, I was relieved to see that all traces of Eric were gone except our shared dresser and an automated trash receptacle he had recently purchased. He had sent me multiple messages urging me to talk, but I had

had nothing to say. As I settled into my half-empty home, I let the full wave of emotions I had felt on the journey back take over me. I wept for my losses (both Guillaume and Eric), I wept for my karma, and I wept for the lack of direction my future held.

I heard a knock on the door and found a woman I did not know standing before me. She knew my name and urged that we speak inside. She introduced herself as Mathy, but it wasn't until she mentioned Eric that I understood why she was there. I let her in despite the utter repulsion I felt. I was defeated and hollow, and whatever I had already endured had hurt enough. There was nothing this woman could say or do that could break me down further.

We sat down around the dining table, and after a moment of silence, she led the conversation with an apology. She told me she felt horrible for wrecking our future. She had met Eric a few years ago, right after he and I had started dating seriously. She had been in love with him ever since, and while they had innocently flirted in the first few months, she had known he was madly in love with me.

As I stared out the window to a grey sky, she explained that it was only about a year ago that she had finally professed her love to him. They worked together, she explained, and it was when he had been let go that she realized she couldn't bare to not see him every day. He had reciprocated her feelings, and they saw each other every day if possible. He had broken it off with her about three weeks ago, saying that their relationship had caused ours far too much strain. I laughed, but without responding or stopping she continued. He had really loved me. And it wasn't until I had been unfaithful that he had returned to her and told her that she was the one he really needed to be with for the rest of his life. She had waited for him, she said, to move in with him. But he never did.

I assumed this to be when he had come back to me, but in my state of complete emptiness, I said nothing. She explained how she begged him to come back to her, and that when I had finally left for my retreat, he had agreed to meet, only to end things. She had been the one to call me. Seeing my missed calls and voicemails show up on his phone, her jealousy had gotten the best of her. Without ever having met me, she had wanted to cause me pain. They had both drank a lot in an effort to drown the pain of goodbye, and when he had given in to her seductions and returned to her apartment, she had stolen his phone and called me to ensure I would hear what had followed. I looked at her for the first time since she had begun speaking to me. Her eyes were red, she had tears running down her face and a rage I had not seen before. She hated that he still loved me; that he had left her once again because of what I had caused her to do.

This woman had loved Eric since she had met him, and she had done everything in her power to be his. Knowing full well that he had loved me and had every intention of marrying me, she had been relentless in her pursuit of him. I knew that kind of love. I had finally experienced that kind of love. And so, I didn't hate her. What I felt for her was a great deal of pain, of understanding. I wanted her to know, and yet, my words failed me.

She got up suddenly, and when did, she asked me if I was happy. I had hurt the man whom she had loved more than anyone she had ever met. He had loved me unconditionally. Yes, he had been unfaithful, but even in his infidelity I was forever present. She told me she knew that when he made love to her, he thought of me. That when he told her she was beautiful, he only saw my face. I had cost her everything she cherished most and with nothing to show for it.

Still at a loss for words, I walked to the door and held it open for her. She walked out quietly, still in tears, and the last words she said to me were that she hoped I was happy. I had destroyed two lives, Eric's and hers. I shut the door behind her and headed straight to my bed. I stripped the sheets and replaced them with new ones, hoping never to feel a trace of Eric again.

CHAPTER TWO

Every day since then has been a blur. I missed work too often. I drank to excess each night. I sat in my chair by the fire for hours without food or water. Days went by before I realized I hadn't showered. I didn't leave the house except to buy more alcohol. I had lost a significant amount of weight, and I had lost all touch with the outside world. When I did go to work, I was mentally absent, failing to cover an entire lesson plan and never fully answering any questions. I was handed written warnings of unacceptable behavior multiple times. After that, I vaguely remember being placed on an improvement plan; I failed. Before I knew it, I received a notice to let me know I had been let go.

In a last ditch effort to redeem myself, I had called my family. I had told them what had happened; Eric had been unfaithful, I had asked him to leave, and I needed their support. I moved back to Grenoble with my family, and there I spent another few months in a state of immobility in every sense of the word. Nothing moved, physically or emotionally. Only basic needs took me places, and aside from the bare minimum needed to survive I kept to myself. My family grew more and more concerned, and eventually forced me to see a therapist.

As the air turned crisp and the leaves started to fall, I remembered a night where it all culminated to a morbid halt. My gloom had grown so dark that I had decided there was no value in continuing on. I was alive, sure, but I wasn't living; not even a little bit. I consumed an entire bottle of painkillers until I felt nothing, and frankly, that was the best I had felt in months. The next thing I remembered was waking up to bright lights flashing by as I was being hauled on a gurney somewhere. The only face I could see with Guillaume's, but I knew he wasn't with me.

GUILLAUME

CHAPTER ONE

I packed up the last of my belongings. In just an hour, my new tenant would be coming by to do a final walk through of the apartment and dropping off some of his things after signing the year-long lease. That night, I would be headed to Bar WINDO to get a final glimpse of Paris' beauty as I said goodbye to the people I had worked closely with for the past few years. The next day, I would be headed to Switzerland to spend a few weeks with my family before heading to my final destination. I exited the metro station at Neuilly Porte Maillot and walked to the Hyatt hotel where the bar was located. As I walked in, I saw my coworkers, balloons in hand, cheering. We took the elevator up to the thirty-fourth floor and checked in with the hostess. She walked us to our table, one with a splendid view of Paris, and as the Eiffel Tower sparkled in the distance, the emotion of what I was leaving behind finally engulfed me.

Paris had been home to so many experiences. Young and undeterred, I had excelled in my studies with relentless ambition to be a data scientist back when data wasn't even a thing. After years of exhausting nights and weekends, I had earned my masters with honors, where I had met the woman who had broken me. She had promised a future of wonders but had treated me like I meant nothing. I had stuck around, hoping for her validation and approval, only to find that she had fallen in love with some image of me, one that I would never be able to uphold. I had then decided to put my career at the forefront and pursued a second masters in teaching at La Sorbonne. Post-graduation, I was hired on for research. There I had found love and lost it just as quickly. Only this time, I had finally understood what my first love had taught me; not all that glitters is gold, and what we dream love will be is often a fleeting illusion. As this revelation settled in, I made my peace with the agony that was Hélène.

The server, approaching with our drinks, broke my train of thought, and I caught the tail end of my coworkers' conversations. Something about a fellow professor having a mental breakdown and losing her job. I felt my heart sink, and as my inquisitive nature demanded, I probed them for her name. As soon as they confirmed it was her, I felt guilty. I asked them if they knew what had caused this, and one of my coworkers mentioned apparently she had simply "gone crazy". In utter disbelief, I told them I needed to head home. Disappointed that the night had been cut short, they insisted I stay a bit longer, but I begged them to stay and continue without me. I made a joke about them sharing nice things about me behind my back, paid for my barely sipped drink and took off. I didn't know where I was headed, or even how to find her, but I knew I had to try.

CHAPTER TWO

I had been lucky enough to catch her last name: Dubois. I knew she lived in the eleventh district, so I looked up an e-directory once I got home. I found a residential phone number and dialed it immediately. Someone picked up, and when I asked for Hélène, they seemed confused. I asked for the owner of the apartment, and they mentioned she had moved to Grenoble. After the call ended, I took a moment to think through things, as had become my habit. If I looked for and found her now, I would have broken my promise. I would have put aside our dreams to ease my guilt. But I also knew that while I had been able to find my path to growth, hers had deteriorated. Whether it was Eric or me, I did not know. All I knew was that the woman I loved, and possibly always would, had lost everything she had cherished. Her job, her love, her home. With how much she loved Paris, there was no way she would have left it to go back home except as a last resort.

I searched for the Dubois family in Grenoble and was inundated with search results. Seeing as how it was already late, I decided to save my calls for the next day, when I would be at home in Switzerland. My guilt, coupled with concern, cost me sleep the entire night. I tossed and turned, and as the hours passed, I felt more and more hopeless. I knew I couldn't move to Amsterdam or possibly even Switzerland without knowing if she was alright. I needed to know the reason she had lost her job, and the reason she had left Paris. Finally, I needed to know my part in all of it.

Different scenarios flashed through my head. In one, she was an alcoholic who had lost everything too quickly to recover. In another, she had fallen terribly ill and had been taken to Grenoble by her family. In yet a third, her experiences in Paris had broken her, and having lost her job, the only option she had had was to move back home. In each situation, I only saw her helpless face. I only saw despair and defeat. I tried to imagine what she had felt, at each pivotal loss of the things she had cherished. I had already been there for the first, and given her reaction, I feared what the rest had done to her. To be honest, I didn't even know if she was still alive. I shivered at the thought that she may have given up hope entirely, and when I glanced at the clock, realized it was already time to get ready for my flight to Switzerland.

HÉLÈNE

CHAPTER ONE

I really thought I had succeeded in taking all of my pain away. I thought I had finally found some peace in leaving my wretched life behind. It wasn't until the next day, when I woke to my family surrounding me, that I knew I had failed. Disappointed, I put on a brave face and made a joke about how weak the pain pills were. Unamused and worried, they begged me to continue resting. Days turned into weeks and months; I never knew where the time went and yet every day was painfully slower than the last. This was yet another thing at which I had failed. Seeing the wreck I had created around me, I promised myself change. This wasn't my first attempt at ending my life, but it would be my last. I had to stop hurting the people around me, and while the two men I had quite possibly loved the most were gone, my family had stuck by me.

I spent a lot of time with my grandparents. Grandma had practically taken me under her wing, constantly checking in and inviting me to her house each weekend. Grandpa and she lived with my uncle, his wife, and my two young cousins in a beautiful property just outside the city. At the slightest indication of a warm day, grandma and I would set up lawn chairs in the lush green fields of the property, silently reading next to each other.

When it was cold, we would sit inside, huddled by the fire. She sat on the rocking chair (her favorite piece of furniture) while I sat on the chaise lounge facing her. When we weren't reading, I was usually sharing with her what I had read or learning about her incredible life and all she had endured. One day, while I was reading Le Grand Secret by Barjavel, I found grandma staring at me pensively. I closed my book and smiled at her, but she seemed sad. When I asked what was on her mind, she sighed deeply.

"My dear, when I look at you, I see shadows of my youth. What times we lived in back then! Two wars, an economic depression and a husband who didn't want to marry me."

At this, I laughed and asked her to explain what she had meant. Her expression changed immediately; there was a hint of mischief in her eyes, which I found incredibly endearing.

"Well, you see, your grandpa and I were family friends. Our parents had always hoped we would get together, but I found him to be rather arrogant, and he found me dull. When he turned eighteen and I sixteen, his father demanded he get married within the year. Not having any other prospects, your grandpa told his father he was ready to marry me, but in return he wanted this land we're sitting on. His father agreed, and we began preparing for the wedding. I was hesitant, you see. I still wasn't very fond of him, and he seemed as disinterested as ever. I tried reasoning with my parents, but they knew his family well and assured me I would feel welcomed. I gave up hope and did as I was told. The day of the wedding came sooner than any of us had expected, but your grandpa was nowhere to be found. So, your great grandpa went in search of him, and found him hiding in one of the rooms at the factory where he worked. Legend has it your great grandpa yanked his ear and dragged him all the way over here that way."

I let out a hearty laugh, and I remembered how long it had been since I had felt that genuinely happy. Grandma continued.

"We got married to the right, just over there." She pointed to an opening where a bed of roses lay in planters. "We spent the first three months of our marriage barely speaking with one another. Then he went to war, and I was heartbroken. I had no one but his family, and I wasn't close with any of them. As little as we spoke, he was the only friend I had in my new home. I was terrified; I didn't know if he would ever come back, and what would happen to me then? Lady Luck was on my side. He came back two years later, and in the meantime, we had been writing to one another. With every letter our bond grew stronger. I had a reason to stay, and he had a reason to come home. We had children right away, and that changed everything. We now had a common enemy, you see!"

She laughed when she said this, as did I. We sat there giggling for a long time, and then her look turned serious.

"I know at times it seems life isn't worth living. Believe me, I know how that feels. When your grandpa was away at war, I thought about what I would do if he didn't come back. The thought crossed my mind, not because I was particularly unhappy, but because I had no purpose. Over the years, I had let all of my dreams slip away from me. Did you know I wanted to be a nurse when I was younger?"

I shook my head to indicate I didn't.

"Ah, well I did. But I grew up in a time where a woman's only job was to get married and have children. I've never regretted my decision to have children because in them, I found my purpose. Before you think I'm suggesting marriage and children for you, let me say this. I'm not. I'm only reminding you how important it is to have a purpose, whatever it may be. I know you loved that job, and it's never too late to go back. Purpose is what drives us, and if there's one thing I've learned, it's to find it sooner rather than later. I'm lucky to have lived a full life, but to think you may have..."

At this, she choked, and tears filled her eyes as they did mine. She was right; I had had so much purpose when I had first moved to Paris. I knew what I wanted to do and where I wanted to be in life. My students had been my whole world, years before I had even met Eric or Guillaume. Why I had let that vision escape me was incomprehensible, but I knew I needed to find my way back. Grandma's kindness and comfort had offered me therapeutic relief, and with my newfound clarity, I felt inspired to piece my life back together.

I applied for and obtained a teaching assistant position at Stendhal. Albeit a step back, I took great comfort in knowing that I wasn't completely unemployable. I worked part-time, and when I was free, I visited grandma and read. The only thing that made me happy those days was her company. I read the classics, modern fiction and, of course, my favorite, sci-fi. I would tell her about the things I read, and she was constantly amused by how animated I was when sharing some of them. Anything that transported me to another world was welcomed, but the more unrealistic, the better. Idle time had become my enemy. Any time I was idle, my mind wandered to Guillaume, and I couldn't bear the thoughts that filled my head.

I wondered if he was still in Paris or if he had moved to Switzerland. I dreaded the thought of it but was curious to know if he had met someone else. I also wished I knew if I would ever see him again. Despite arduous efforts to distract myself and divert these thoughts, idle time found me. Whether it was in the shower or the walk to the tram stop, I couldn't escape it. In those moments, I was profoundly miserable and dark thoughts managed to creep in. I eventually made friends at the university, and the lone walk to the metro stop had become a walk with several coworkers. Mundane as the conversations could be at times, they redirected my attention to simpler things.

After a year on the road to recovery, my family brought up the painful topic of meeting someone. Although Grenoble was fairly small in comparison to Paris, they had insisted there were plenty of opportunities for a single woman. They suggested I go out with my friends after work from time to time, or even venture back to Paris with my sister for one weekend each month. I knew their intentions were centered around my well-being, but the thought of returning to Paris fueled my anxiety. Unable to breathe, I always left the room in tears. After a few months of failed attempts, they stopped asking.

CHAPTER TWO

One night, I woke up to the sound of my phone buzzing. I answered to find my cousin crying hysterically, letting me know grandma had passed in her sleep. To say my world was shattered would have been an understatement. Not even the loss of Eric or Guillaume had left me this shaken. The shock absorbed me the entire night, and I found myself unable to shed any tears. I headed to my grandparents' house the next day, where concerned family members asked me repeatedly if I was going to be alright.

I had loved this woman so deeply, and to some extent, I had taken her for granted for so long. I hardly ever visited when I was in Paris, and the few weekends I had managed to come to Grenoble, visiting her was only an option if I didn't have much else to do. Guilt enveloped me, and as everyone around me sobbed, I envied their ability to express their grief. For me, the tears wouldn't come. Thinking a few drinks may open up the floodgates, I headed to the local bar and ordered one martini after another. Drunk and barely able to walk, I felt emptier inside than when I had first walked in.

Devoid of any emotion, I said goodbye to grandma. I remembered my summers with her when I was a little girl, and painfully, I remembered the last few months with her. She had helped me find peace, even a kind of happiness. Most of all, she had reminded me of my purpose. Without having to tell her how I felt or what I had been through, she had given me exactly what I had needed. Kindness. Love. Unconditional comfort. Knowing I would never have that again broke my heart, and yet, on the surface, I looked unmoved.

I visited her grave often. They had buried her on the property, and I went every weekend. I listened to grandpa share stories of when they had been young; how they had married, her letters to him during the war, how happy they had been to see each other when he had come back. I heard my uncle talk about her life, about the strength she had exemplified, even when they had had nothing. Especially when they had nothing. How she had sacrificed her own meals to ensure that her children never went hungry, how she was always the last to eat once everyone else had had a chance to grab seconds.

In the months that followed her passing, I never once thought of Guillaume. It wasn't until eight months later, when the professor whom I had been helping had shared an article about Bern that he finally came to mind. As quickly as he had come to mind, he had gone away. Death of a loved one provides perspective. Mine had taught me that what I thought of as love had not been close to the love I had actually lost. The love I had lost through no fault of my own, through no excuses guised as promises of an unforeseen future and the love of fate. What I had lost had been taken from me unwillingly, and the ashes of memories that I carried reminded me of this continually.

CHAPTER THREE

A few weeks later, my long lost love of Paris rose sleepily from its seemingly endless slumber. The feeling overwhelmed me, and I told my family I would be spending the weekend in Paris. I had already booked my train ticket and hotel room, and I wanted to go alone. In fact, I needed to go alone. Not willing to burden any of my family members with the potential breakdown I could have when I got there, I insisted I was finally ready to face the ghosts of my past. The train ride was excruciating; my mind wandered in several directions. From running into old coworkers, Guillaume or Eric to what I would visit first, I barely noticed the three hours coming to an abrupt halt at Gare du Nord. I took my bag off of the rack as I exited the compartment and walked to the exit. Not wanting to lug my suitcase around, I found a taxi out front and headed to the hotel Les Plumes.

I had been lucky; the Rimbaud/ Verlaine room had been available, and as I rode the elevator up to the third floor, the exhaustion of the last few months finally caught up with me. For the first time in a long time, I can honestly say I had fallen asleep by the time my head hit the pillow. I woke up several hours later to the sun beating down on Paris. Wanting to take advantage of the nice weather, I decided a bit of flânerie was in order. I exited the hotel and wandered with no destination in mind. I did this for about an hour and ended up at a small bar-tabac, where I bought a pack of Gauloises and ordered an espresso. I sat in the covered patio and watched passers-by, and with no warning or trigger, the tears I had been unable to shed for months finally rose to the surface.

Embarrassed and unwilling to sob in public, I quickly paid my tab and exited the bar. I hailed a taxi on the main street and headed back to the hotel. There, in utter seclusion, I allowed the fury of my emotions to take me on whatever adventure they had planned. I cried for hours, for my sweet grandmother who was taken from me too soon, for her beautiful life that had touched so many of us, for the warm embraces I would never again experience and for all the love I had lost. The only thing I had known since I was young had been sheer disappointment. Nothing good had ever lasted, and I had convinced myself it never would.

At some point, I had fallen asleep, and when I finally woke up, I was stuffy and red-eyed, and quite frankly, an absolute mess. I decided to take a shower and decompress, letting the hot water consume me. It was a cleansing of my past, of my soul, of my mind. I was slowly letting go of the brokenness and pain I had kept so close to me all this time. The pain that had never left my side had befriended me, and if I were ever to be happy, truly happy, I would have to let it go. I thought of Guillaume. I had been afraid to let go of the pain his memories brought back because after all, the pain was all I had of him. Letting go of the pain had meant letting go of him, and until now, I hadn't been ready.

CHAPTER FOUR

As my tears mixed with the water, one now indistinguishable from the other, I felt a weight leave my shoulders. I had held onto so much for so long, I had hardly noticed how slouchy and small it had me. For the first time for as long as I could remember, I stood tall and upright. I finished my shower and got ready to face more demons from my past. I headed to the eleventh district and sat down at L'Artiste with a fresh pack of Gauloises and a collection of Rimbaud's letters. Ordering my once regular vegetarian sandwich and glass of Chinon, I tried to decipher the words Rimbaud had etched in his letters to various mentors and renowned poets. I felt reconnected with a part of me I had almost forgotten; the part that had loved poetry to pieces and cried at the beauty words could hold. I stopped to eat my dinner and resumed reading with a fresh cigarette and refilled glass of wine. An hour later, I decided to take the metro back home.

I took a detour around the eleventh district to get to the Voltaire stop; I had missed my neighborhood more than I could have imagined. It felt like I had never left, and yet, this version of me had never been here before. I knew in that instant I would have to come home, and that I would have to do it soon. To elaborate on the moveable feast Hemingway had called Paris, if you had spent any time of your youth in Paris, and a considerable amount of time at that, it never left you. And no matter where in the world you ventured thereafter, Paris went with you. He was right. I felt this now more than ever before, and every part of my soul ached to come back. This was my home; this was where I belonged, and no humiliating memories or past mistakes would keep me from it anymore.

Despite having done little besides sleep the whole day, I fell asleep almost immediately upon my return to Les Plumes. I slept soundly and dreamt vividly of grandma, of her laughter as I shared yet another ridiculous zombie apocalypse story with her. I woke up with tears in my eyes, but for once, there was no pain. There was a longing, sure, but not the same pain that had been incessantly brewing within me for the past few years. I spent the next morning at Père Lachaise, wandering for hours. I visited Piaf, Éluard and Chopin along with a host of unknowns who had been laid to rest in its beautiful grounds. Afterwards, I had another lunch at L'Artiste and headed straight to Notre-Dame to spend my afternoon reading at Shakespeare & Co. I sat upstairs, petting Aggie and continuing my journey through Rimbaud's youth. After a successful day of reconnecting with my home, I headed to a nearby café for dinner before returning to the hotel.

CHAPTER FIVE

The next day was painful to say the least. I said a teary-eyed goodbye to Paris as I boarded my train back to Grenoble. Worried I would've wanted to leave quickly, I had chosen an earlier departure, which I regretted. Exhausted from the emotional toll saying goodbye had taken on me, I fell asleep. I woke up to find only an hour of my journey remained. In this time, I plugged in my headphones and listened to music, gazing at the scenery we left behind. My family warily asked me questions about my weekend. They didn't dare venture into how I was doing, but instead asked me what I enjoyed the most, where I ate, or what I visited while I was there. I answered their questions cheerfully and broke the news that I would start applying to jobs in Paris the very next day. I had decided to go back home, and while I knew they worried, they were extremely supportive of my decision.

I applied to several schools and universities, and thanks to the marvelous recommendation my hosting professor in Grenoble had provided, I was offered a probationary position at La Sorbonne as an assistant. Despite my pitiful departure from the school, the dean had remembered me and had been kind enough to fight for me when I had reapplied.

She had called me personally to let me know and had expressed her utmost condolences for what I had gone through in the last few months I had been there. I noticed the catch in her throat when she shared her sadness for the loss of my grandmother. Ecstatic that I would be able to start teaching that summer, I broke the news to my tenant that she would need to move out by the end of May. Unhappy with the suddenness of my request, she told me she may need some more time. Finding an apartment in Paris wasn't exactly the easiest of tasks, and given only one month remained, it would be difficult to find something that quickly.

Knowing full well what I was burdening her with, I agreed to stay at a hotel if she had still not found accommodations by the time I was prepared to leave Grenoble. As a bit of incentive, I wrote her a glowing recommendation that boasted her timeliness with rent and her overall demeanor, making her an excellent tenant. Luck was with me, for only five days later, she called to confirm she had found another apartment, and my flat would be ready by the time I arrived. I spent the last few weeks in Grenoble close to both my immediate and extended family. I made sure to never miss a meal at home, and I spent every weekend with my grandfather, uncle and cousins. I spent an hour each day at my grandmother's grave and continued to share with her the ridiculous adventures of aliens, zombies and all the things that had amused her so.

The last weekend I spent by her side was difficult, but I promised myself I would return once a month to see her.

THE
JOURNEY HOME

CHAPTER ONE

Even with her rejuvenated spirit, Hélène spent many an evening wondering what could have been. There was a day she distinctly remembered, when she had been cleaning the apartment and had found Eric's stash of hot chocolate in a cabinet above the fridge. Ever since her early twenties, having spent much of her youth working at local pâtisseries, she had grown to dislike sweets. He had always loved them, and so he would buy hot chocolate sachets and hide them in places she wasn't bound to look. It was never because she would have gotten angry with him. Over time, this had become something of an amusing surprise whenever she stumbled upon them. They would both laugh when this happened, and she had always found something charming about his game of hide-and-seek-the-hot-chocolate.

Without knowing why, she found herself sobbing. This inevitably led to thoughts about her relationship with Eric, then the relationship she had never had with Guillaume, and all that had and would never happen between them. She remembered the day she had lost both of the men she had loved, in completely different ways, forever. She tried not to think of the promise Guillaume had made her and the possibilities it brought with it, and to let herself feel the pain she did as if all was finished between them. Convincing herself of the fact that it would be just her, possibly until the end of her days, she surrendered herself to the tears.

La Sorbonne was a perfect distraction whenever one of these bouts of depression caught up with her. She worked endless hours, utterly devoted to her students. She stayed at the university library every weeknight, working away until it closed. On the weekends, she would head to the François-Mitterand library to lesson plan and catch up on reading. She rarely spent any time in her apartment, and when she did, she busied herself with cleaning or reading about new and inventive teaching techniques. As long as her mind was elsewhere, she could function.

By now, she had cleaned her apartment several times over, and there were no surprises left to be found. She moved around some of the furniture, changed out her reading chair, bed sheets and comforter, and even replaced the paintings that hung from the wall. The previously Impressionist art that hung around her apartment was now replaced with poems; from Baudelaire to Rimbaud to Yves Bonnefoy, she had found her favorite words and plastered them all over the apartment to remind herself of her first love, poetry.

CHAPTER TWO

The hot chocolate incident had left a wound exposed. Try as she might, Guillaume's thoughts frequented her often, and she found it difficult to expel them. She finally decided she would write him a letter, one expressing all she had felt, and that would decisively state they had no future. So, she wrote.

My dearest Guillaume,

I find it strange to address something to you with my dearest before it, but nothing else seemed right for the purposes of this letter. I have struggled with the thought of you for some time now, and in my hopeless pursuit to forget you, realized that I needed to write out my thoughts so that they would finally be real. If you're reading this standing, I suggest you sit down; this will take some time.

My reasons for this letter are threefold: one, to let you know how grateful I am for all you did for me; two, to let you know what my mind and soul have been through since we parted ways; and finally, three, now that I have had the time to process it, what your parting words mean to me. At times, this will not have a clear stream of consciousness or organization, and I apologize in advance. With all I need to say to you, it's hard to stay focused on one thing at a time.

Before I get to the gut-wrenching portions of this letter, ones that pain me more than you can imagine, I want to thank you. You have taught me such kindness, patience and selflessness. More than anything, you have showed me a kind of maniacal love I didn't think existed. I read about it, sure, even saw it in movies, but I never believed real people could have the sorts of connections that debilitated them. I know I didn't fight for you, and maybe I should have. This is a regret I will carry with me all my life. The regret, to be clear, is not that I didn't fight for you, but that I will never know if I should have. I'm not certain I will ever feel the way I felt with you with anyone else, but I'm also not certain what grounds we would have had for any sort of romantic relationship considering the foundation would have been a betrayal on my end. Back to you though; each time I left and came back, you were there, whether it was to save me, support me, or the very last time, to heal my heart and break it all over again. Be that as it may, in some of my darkest moments, you shared with me your light, and it brought me peace. And for that, I am forever indebted to you.

My mind runs through the one and only night we had together, and the intense passion with which I find myself overcome is hard to describe. I replay those moments in my mind's eye often, and they bring such pain and such comfort. I know we shared that moment, and yet, as time passes, I wonder if I imagined it. In our last conversation, you mentioned *that if the universe ever brought us back together, that you would not fight it. But, I have to know, are you fighting the universe in bringing us to one another again? How is it that we managed to see each other thrice in a span of a year without planning it, but knowing where the other lives and working in the same place I can't find any trace of you? Did you simply say that to appease my already broken heart? Had too much time passed, and had I played with your heart enough for you to think it was time to say goodbye for good?*

Yes, I destroyed you, but could you have imagined yourself in my shoes? What would you have done? I ask myself constantly if I would have changed anything, and I always end up with the answer that I do not know if I could have. Eric and I were going to be married. I had never taken that step with anyone before and had never even shared a home with another man before him. At that time, I did not know of his unfaithfulness, nor could I have imagined it. I knew that losing his job had turned him cold and ruthless at times, but never once did I suspect that he could have hurt me in the way he did. This, for all I knew, was my future. And then you came along to save me, and everything I thought I knew instantly became blurry. Would you have risked everything you already had for something you had barely gotten the chance to explore?

I ask you these questions because the words you said to me when I last shared the same space with you have finally had a chance to simmer. Was it I who broke you, or was it something else? I often wonder if the fact that I was unattainable made me more interesting to you. Believe me, it wouldn't be the first time. As I go through some shame in asking you this, I have to know. Did you ever feel what I felt? Or was it just a phase that ended, and seeing that I was already crushed, you found a way to leave me without ever revealing your true intentions? I may never know the answer to this, and maybe you'd be offended by the questions. I can't tell you how many times I'm going to reread this, and how many times I will go through this whirlwind of emotions.

After losing Eric and you, I lost everything. My despair got the best of me, and I saw my life slip away. I moved back to Grenoble, and there I found solace in the wonderful being that was my grandmother. She gave me hope, hope that I could be happy again, that I could find my way again. I started to work, and eventually found my way back to Paris and La Sorbonne. The traces of the existence I once had slowly but surely began to reappear. But my growth came at a huge price. I lost her unexpectedly, and it devastated me. While she was the one who had pushed me to come back, to return to the person I used to be, to find my passions and purpose again, she took a big part of me with her. And as I slowly picked up the pieces of my broken life, the glue that was holding me together was gone.

Some days, I find it surprising that I'm still here. I'm not saying this to elicit pity or sympathy from you. I'm saying it because it made me think of you and of us. Losing her reminded me of the time we have in this world, and how quickly it can be taken from us. I'm happy she lived as full a life as she possibly could have, but tomorrow, one of us could be taken and then there would be no universe bringing us back together. I found myself wondering why you would put such a stipulation on us if you really felt what I had felt. Sure, I needed to officially end things with Eric, and sure, I would have probably needed some time to gather myself. But could you not have hung on a bit longer?

This is where I go back to wondering if I imagined it. But your words remind me that I didn't, or at least they didn't lead me to believe I did. In your words, which I could repeat verbatim, you expressed what I had been feeling towards you more perfectly than I could have done. I felt the same desire, the same anguish, the same yearning you had felt. And I felt your pain, I felt the hurt I had caused you, and the destruction I had brought to us, albeit unintentional and difficult to avoid as I have stated above. So why did you make the decision to end us? This question circles my mind often, and I know the only way I will find closure and be able to move on is if I can understand just what it is that you felt. Not in that moment, but for me, in all of the time you knew me. Did you really feel the way it seemed you did?

I'll leave you with just these last thoughts: if I had known my fate with Eric and had your intentions been as they seemed, I would have fought the world for you. I've often thought about apologizing to you for not fighting for you, but it's not so much an apology as it is regret that I couldn't have changed anything. And I suppose now, I won't know if I even should have. I only want to know, if in return, what you felt was real, sincere and honest, or if I had fallen prey to some twisted form of projection. It's no surprise then, that your thoughts bring me pain, joy, sorrow, regret, anger and confusion. I hope that wherever you are, you're finding happiness. I hope someday I will too. As for your promise, I want no part of it anymore. If by some miracle, you let the universe bring us back together, I can no longer afford myself the luxury of an open heart. My wounds may never heal, but I refuse to reopen them or the past that broke me and rendered me irreparable.

Sincerely,
Hélène

She never sent the letter. While she remembered his address and knew she could have easily mailed it to him or found a way to send it his way on campus, she simply wanted her words to make it out of her head. Over time, his thoughts lessened in gravity, and she was able to function most days without something reminding her of him. Imaginably impossible considering they had met where she spent five out of the seven days in a week, Hélène managed quite well as time progressed.

CHAPTER THREE

Eight months later, Hélène received a phone call from her former tenant. Surprised to hear from her, Hélène answered, wondering if she was simply looking for a contact who could help her find a place. The girl mentioned that someone had dropped off a letter for Hélène, and that while she had fully intended to mail it, she had forgotten and stowed it away. She found it recently when she went through the last of her boxes of souvenirs and letters.

She promised to come by the next day and drop it off as she would be in the ninth district. Surprised to have received a letter while in Grenoble, Hélène agreed to meet her in the morning for a coffee so they could catch up. She had always felt badly about demanding her apartment back at such short notice, and so Hélène felt she had owed her at least a cup of coffee, if not more. Considering it had now nearly a year since she had been back and even longer since the letter may have first arrived, she knew it couldn't have been anything urgent. She went to bed, and as had been the case lately, was sound asleep in seconds.

The next morning, she walked over to L'Artiste for her rendez-vous. They grabbed espressos and spent most of the time talking about their lives for the past couple of years. Two hours flew by, and when her tenant mentioned she had another engagement, they called for the check. Hélène paid, glad to be able to do it, and accepted the long-lost letter as they said their goodbyes. Hélène opened up the letter as soon as she got home. There was no name on the envelope, it was sans address, and she realized whoever wrote it would have hand delivered it.

Her heart once again fell to the pit of her stomach as her eyes skimmed the note to find the signature at the end:

My Hélène,

I know I have no right to call you mine anymore, but I hope you will at least read this. I asked around about you and heard the terrible news about La Sorbonne. I know how much you loved what you did, and I'm so sorry to hear what happened. I can't help but blame myself; if I hadn't done what I did, we would still be happy together. You would still have your job, I would have mine, and we would have been married. It pains me to think of what we could have had; every day begins and ends with the depressing thought that I broke us.

I'm writing to you because I know you won't take my calls or see me. Without you, my life is empty. I'm not like you, and words aren't my strong suit, but I need you to know how terribly sorry I am for my infidelity. You had always been so patient with me, so kind even when I wasn't, so loving even when I didn't deserve it. I never deserved you, and I know I still don't. I didn't love her the way I did you; in fact, I could never love someone the way I did and still love you. You're the love of my life, and even now, I won't stop hoping we can talk.

I'm writing to ask you if you'd be willing to give me a chance. I'm not saying we should rush back into anything; I wouldn't ask or expect that of you. I'm simply saying that maybe, just maybe, we could start over with a friendship and build trust over time. I know it's hard to rebuild, and you may have already moved on, but I can't seem to shake the feeling that we both think back to what we had. I love you, my Hélène, my sweet, beautiful Hélène, and I can't go on pretending life is worth living without you. I have not stopped thinking about you, and as we always tend to realize what we have once it's gone, that's exactly how I feel.

If there is any chance that you could let me back into your life, even just as a friend, I would be so happy. I miss our friendship more than anything. Yes, we had romance, but at the core of what we were was this friendship that made us better. We laughed, we cried, we shared our hopes and dreams and supported each other. Sure, I failed at times, but we both cared so deeply about the other, and I find it hard to believe that it just goes away. Especially after the number of years we had together, and the home we shared. Hopefully you understand how I feel, and as unrealistic as it is on my part, that you share the sentiment.

I'll wait for your reply, indefinitely. If not now, if years from now you choose to find me, I'll be here. I love you my Hélène; I always have, and I always will. I hope you know that, and above all, I hope you're happy wherever you are.

Yours forever,

Eric

Hélène felt sad for Eric; somewhere, he had been hoping she would reply. Much like the days when he realized he had been wrong and waited for her to come home so he could apologize, he must have been waiting for her to respond. She must have seemed cruel for never having written back, even if it was to say they couldn't be friends. Maybe he thought she had found love and forgotten all about him. Her empathy for him wore her down, but she knew she would never be able to move on if she didn't leave her past behind her.

She decided to write back at the address he had left under his name. She chose each word carefully, ensuring he didn't feel like her lack of response was malicious, born out of her need to see him be tortured. For the first time in a long time, there were no tears, just a sense of peace for what she was about to do:

Dear Eric,

First and foremost, I apologize for my delay in responding to you. I've been in Grenoble for some time now and just received this letter today as my former tenant had accidentally stored it with her belongings. Had I known you had written to me, I would have surely responded. I also want to thank you. I know it couldn't have been easy to write this, especially not knowing if or when I would respond; I'm inspired by your courage.

I'm touched by your letter, and you are right in saying that you don't forget about people or what you shared so easily. It also puts a smile on my face to think about our friendship. I remember the great times we shared as friends above all else, and I will treasure these fond memories all my life. You were the best friend a girl could have had, and I am so grateful for that.

As to the question of us reconnecting, I'm afraid too much has passed to allow for that. I promise that I have forgiven you. As much time and pain as it has taken for me to get here, it has given me peace to finally let go of the hostility, shame and hurt I once felt when I thought of you, of how we ended. We have definitely been through a lot together, and as much as our friendship means the world to me, it is but a memory that I hold. Anything further, I would not be able to give.

I want you to be happy, and as much as I didn't think I could be someday, I know there is still hope.

I'm sure you'll meet someone, and even if it is her, I wish you two nothing but the best. I've often believed that sometimes we are in someone's life momentarily for a reason, whether it's for a few weeks or a few years. I feel the same for us. We both gave each other so much, and it is more than enough for one lifetime. Reopening old wounds or trying to rekindle something that isn't there anymore would do us more harm than good, this much I can assure you.

I mean it when I say I wish you well. In fact, I wish you all the happiness I could never give you. I know the universe has better things in store for you. I hope you will find it in your heart to forgive me for the things I did, and that you'll forgive me above all else for not fulfilling the request in your letter. Someday, you'll be thankful for this decision, however heartbreaking and torturous it may seem at the moment.

Please remember that I loved you once, deeply, and that you have given me so much happiness. Though not in the same way as before, I will keep you in my heart for the days to come and continue to wish you all the happiness in the world.

Best wishes,
Hélène

She had managed, in the span of a week, to make peace with closing the doors to Eric and Guillaume permanently. Although Hélène did not send Guillaume the letter she wrote to him, she knew her mind had eased knowing her thoughts had been penned down and her questions released to a piece of paper she could re-read whenever she felt uneasy.

The tears for Guillaume also eventually stopped. Work continued to consume her, and it had been almost a year since her job had been considered secure by the university. At last, it seemed to Hélène, the pieces of her life were slowly coming back together. They would surely never be the same, but at the very least, this gave her some measure of comfort and security, something she hadn't had for a long time.

CHAPTER FOUR

Despite the assurance the permanency of her job offered, Hélène's attitude did not change. She worked harder than ever, and continued to keep her mind occupied, mostly for fear of regression to her era of love and loss. One winter night, like every other of the past year and a half, she packed up and left the library rather late. As she began her walk to the train station, she fidgeted through her bag to find her metro tickets. Distracted, she lost track of the general direction, took a wrong turn and ended up in a dark alley she didn't recognize. She knew it couldn't be a good sign that no one was around and panicked as she tried to reorient herself.

She stopped to take out her phone as she reminded herself that she would be out on to the main street in minutes. After all, she had barely begun walking, and the university wasn't far away if she needed help. Just then, she heard a noise behind her. Startled by the sudden disruption of the silence, she turned around to find three men leering at her and cat-calling as they stumbled in her direction.

She started to walk while still digging through her bag, but before she could get very far, a fourth man appeared out of a corner in front of her and stopped her dead in her tracks. Her mind raced, trying to figure out how she could escape, but with crushing despair, she realized she was trapped. The only tool she had at her disposal was her bag full of books, and as she calmed herself, she reminded herself that she could hit the lone fourth man with her bag and run before the others could catch up. A light drizzle had begun by now, and she thought about how useful her umbrella would have been given her situation.

The three approached slowly but surely, laughing and making lewd remarks. She decided she needed to take her shot then and there. She lifted her bag to hurl it at the fourth man, but before she could make impact, he caught on to her intentions and moved aside. Coming up behind her, he grabbed her in a chokehold while the other three ran towards her. One of them pulled out a knife, and she realized what she was facing. There would be no use fighting. She let her body go limp, and the fourth man laughed at the fact that she had conceded.

As tears filled her eyes, and she shut them to prepare for the worst, she heard a voice call out to the men from a distance. She thought it sounded like a policeman but second-guessing the luck that was hardly ever on her side, she dismissed it to either another one of their gang, or simply a passerby who would be unable to fight off four strong men. She was surprised when the thugs suddenly pushed her aside and ran off with a start. They must have also thought he was a policeman, she realized, and slowly got up off of the ground. During her fall, she had scraped her right knee, the same one that had barely recovered a year ago from her tumble down the stairs.

The rain had picked up and she was reminded of all the storms she had weathered thus far. Grateful to have survived this one, she turned around to face the policeman and thank him. Picking up her bag and brushing the dirt off of her coat, she smiled at him. He hadn't changed a bit; he stared at her with the same grey eyes, the same cool appearance, the same tall, slender frame and fitted shirt that revealed the perfect figure underneath.

The first of the two to speak, she asked, "why is it that you're always the one to either save me or destroy me?"

THE END
(FOR NOW...)

ACKNOWLEDGEMENTS

If you can believe it, this is the hardest for me to write. I am one of the luckiest souls in the world, for the people around me are absolute angels. I'll do my best to cover everyone, but those within me who have left my life shall remain unnamed. They are still a big part of this, bigger than anyone can imagine, but if I went down that rabbit hole I could write a whole novel.

To my family: you are the core of my being.

Mom and Papa: Thank you for always believing in me and supporting my dreams. I've made a lot of mistakes in my life and stumbled along the way, but your diligence, persistence and patience have left me with lessons for which I am incredibly thankful. You are amazing, and I hope I make you proud. I love you.

Palomi: Bacchlu, you are my best friend. I'm so grateful for your constant support and encouragement, especially through writing this novel. I'm glad we've gotten through everything we've encountered, and our bond is one I cherish deeply. Thank you for designing my beautiful cover (and the covers to come); there's no one more talented and filled with unlimited potential than you in my world. I love you.

Arpit and Amber: Your journeys and your love are an inspiration. I'm so motivated by how hard you both work and so grateful for the support you've provided in my most dire times. I thank you most for all of the prayers you've kept me in when I couldn't see an end in sight. I love you.

Bai: There was no way I was going to write my story without you in it. I miss you every day. You've always been and will be another mother to me, and I wish you could be here in person. I know you're always with us, and your guiding light has been my strength in the darkest of times. I love you.

Bapa: My bosom buddy! Your grace, kindness and love have always been pillars of strength for us, and I have cherished every moment I've spent with you. I wouldn't be who I am today without you. I hope you will come see us again soon. I love you.

Shraddha: Thank you for being the first non-reader of my first draft and reading it in one sitting. Thank you for always being the most honest version of yourself. A girl can never have enough sisters, and I'm so glad I have you. I know we don't say it to each other, and we don't need to, but I love you.

Priya: Ma sœur! I love that we can have conversations in the Hindi alphabet while actually communicating in French. I love that you've constantly reminded me of the temporary nature of things and believed in me. I'm grateful for the sisterhood we have, and I love the little poet you've created. I love you.

To my friends: I don't know what I would do without you.

Andrew: Thank you for the title of my trilogy. We have weathered quite the storms together, which makes this all the more special. Thank you for your constant love and support, and for the many beautiful memories we have and will continue to make. I love you.

Andre: You are the end all be all of inspiration. I'm glad you're a mission man, because seeing you chase your dreams and work harder than anyone I've ever known motivates me to no end. I miss you so much, but I'm happy to see you doing so well. I love you.

Monica: Where do I even begin? I know you've probably read this and recognized so much of our lives and struggles in this, and I'm so happy you're in my life. You're my other half, my partner-in-crime, and I couldn't imagine this journey without you in it. I love you.

Alton: You are so wonderful, I don't know where to start. I'm so grateful we constantly share our journeys with each other. Your kindness and willingness to help people inspires me to do better. I learn so much from you every day, and you always help me put things into perspective. Thank you, above all else, for pushing me to finish this. I love you.

Olympia: My pineapple! You are so wonderful, sweet and kind. I am so grateful that we share the love of Paris, and one of these days, we are going there together. You and the girls have a special place in my heart, and we shall be Olytiti for years to come. I love you.

Anna: Dix ans! Mais tout ce qu'on a vécu! Je suis trop contente que tu sois dans ma vie. Merci pour tout ce que tu fais, pour ton encouragement pendant les moments difficiles, pour ta tendresse, et surtout, pour ton amitié. Je pense souvent aux deux femmes âgées qu'on avait vu à Reims, et je ris en pensant que ce sera nous un jour. Je t'aime fort ma banane.

Julien: Je suis tellement contente qu'Anna nous ait introduit ; ma vie ne sera pas telle qu'elle est sans toi. Tu es le visage de bonheur, de l'amitié, de l'empathie. On a passé de très bels moments ensemble, et je m'en souviens souvent. Je t'aime fort mon Juju, et à très bientôt!

Sunil: You said it perfectly; I miss having you in my life so much. We're going on 15 years of friendship, and I still can't imagine the last decade and a half without you in it. I can't wait until we are closer, but until then, I have memories enough for a lifetime to remind me of the wonder that you are. I love you.

Hareli: You're my oldest friend, and I'm a better person because of you. I fondly remember our days of French homework and chai, birthday parties and dancing with your dad. We have gone through so much in the two decades we've known each other. I'm amazed by your kindness, patience and unconditional love. I love you.

Rikki: I'm stealing your line, but you're the best thing I got out of grad school. You've given me the one thing I had lost years ago: faith. I look at you and Crystal, the life you're building, the happiness you exude, and I can't help but beam with pride. I thank you for bringing Loan into my life. I love you.

Loan: You are my lobster. I can't believe we went our entire lives without meeting, but I'm glad you're in it now. I am so grateful for the time I get with you and look forward to growing old together. I smile every time I think of you and Thu. I love you.

Julie—Wifey! You have been so kind, amazing, joyous. I'm with my soulmate when I'm with you. Your journey and strength are so inspirational, your love is so magnanimous, and your heart is so pure and kind. I'm one lucky wifey. I love you.

Finally, to my muses and the unnamed: I thank you. Without you, none of this would exist.